53 83 137

A Gifted Earl

Regency Romance

Arietta Richmond

Dreamstone Publishing © 2023

www.dreamstonepublishing.com

ISBN: 978-1-922735-27-0

Disclaimer

Dedication

For everyone who had the grace to be patient while this book, and every other book that I have written, was coming into existence, who provided cups of tea, and food, when the writing would not let me go, and endured countless times being asked for opinions.

For the readers who inspire me to continue writing, by buying my books! Especially for those of you who have taken the time to email me, or to leave reviews, and tell me what you love about my books, and what you'd like to see more of – thank you – I'm listening. I hope that you enjoy this new series (which features some appearances by old favourite characters from the His Majesty's Hounds series), just as much as my other books.

For my growing team of beta readers and advance reviewers – it's thanks to you that others can enjoy these books in the best presentation possible!

And for all the writers of Regency Historical Romance, whose books I read, who inspired me to write in this fascinating period.

Table of Contents

Books by Arietta Richmond

His Majesty's Hounds

Claiming the Heart of a Duke
Giving a Heart of Lace
Enchanting the Duke
Finding the Duke's Heir
Healing Lord Barton
Loving the Bitter Baron
Rescuing the Countess
Attracting the Spymaster
Intriguing the Viscount
Being Lady Harriet's Hero
Redeeming the Marquess
Winning the Merchant Earl
Kissing the Duke of Hearts
Falling for the Earl
Betting on a Lady's Heart
Courting a Spinster for Christmas
Restoring the Earl's Honour
A Scandalous Spring (An additional short story)
The Scent of First Love (an additional short story)
From Soldier Spy to Lord (contains the first three books in one volume)
To Love a Determined Lady (Contains Books 4, 5 and 6 in one volume)
Love Heals a Lord (Contains Books 7, 8 and 9 in one volume)
To Love a Dashing Lord (Contains Books 10, 11, 12, and 13 in one volume)
For a Lady's Honour (Contains Books 14, 15, 16, and 17 in one volume)

A Duke's Daughters – The Elbury Bouquet

A Spinster for a Spy (Lily)
A Bluestocking for a Baron (Rose)
A Minx for a Merchant (Primrose)
A Maiden for a Marquess (Iris)
A Vixen for a Viscount (Hyacinth)
A Diamond for a Duke (Camellia)
An Enchantress for an Earl (Violet)
A Heart for an Heir (Thorne)

The Family Sagas Collections

The Barrington Saga
The Morton Saga
The Dartworth Saga
The Edgeworth Saga
The Windemere Saga
The Chester Saga

The Nettlefold Chronicles

The Duke and the Spinster
A Duke in Autumn
To Wed an Earl
To Dance with the Dangerous Duke
A Christmas Bride for the Duke
The Marquess Elopes
The Scandalous Countess

Lady Canterford's Conspirators (The Mayfair Ladies Poetry Society)

A six book series (coming soon)

The Duke of Traithewood's Legacy

The Marquess Marries a Twin

The Regency Gothic Series

Lord of the Storm
Lord of the Darkness
Lord of the Shadows
Lord of the Lost
Lord of the Betrayed

The Regency Scandals Series

The Gift of a Christmas Scandal
Lady Mariel's Scandalous Love
Christmas with *That* Duke
Lord of Dragons (written with Kyrii Rayne)

The Derbyshire Set

A Gift of Love (Prequel short story)
A Devil's Bargain (Prequel short story - coming soon)
The Earl's Unexpected Bride
The Captain's Compromised Heiress
The Viscount's Unsuitable Affair
The Count's Impetuous Seduction
The Rake's Unlikely Redemption
The Marquess' Scandalous Mistress
The Marchioness' Second Chance
A Viscount's Reluctant Passion
Lady Theodora's Christmas Wish
A Remembered Face (Bonus short story – coming soon)
The Duke's Improper Love (coming soon)
A Gentleman's Unconventional Courtship (coming soon)
The Derbyshire Set, Omnibus Edition, Volume 1 (the first three books in one volume.)
The Derbyshire Set, Omnibus Edition, Volume 2 (the second three books in one volume.)
The Derbyshire Set, Omnibus Edition, Volume 3 (the third three books in one volume.)

Themed Collections

The Regency Christmas Hearts Collection
The Regency Christmas Love Collection
The Regency Spring and Valentine's Hearts Collection
The Regency Summer Hearts Collection
The Regency Autumn Hearts Collection
The Regency Spring Love Collection
The Regency Summer Love collection
Regency Lords in Love
Regency Ladies in Love

The 'Her Duke' Collection

Her Summer Duke
Her Passionate Duke
Her Absent Duke
Her Determined Duke
Her Generous Duke
Her Christmas Duke

Other Books

The Scottish Governess
The Duke's Christmas Vow
Lady Augusta's Letters
A Gifted Earl
The Crew of the Seadragon's Soul Series, (coming soon - a set of 10 linked novels)

Prologue

1814 – Close to a battlefield in France.

"You've a deft hand for it."

The young man tied off the last stitch in the horse's shoulder and looked up, only then becoming consciously aware of the older man who had spoken. He'd been so deeply focused on his task that he'd welcomed the extra hands helping to keep the horse still as he worked, but not thought at all about the person whose hands they were.

He rose, wiping the sweat from his brow, and nodded.

"Thank you for the compliment – and for the steadying hands. There are never enough men about to help – at least not men with enough sympathy for the horses to be useful. The horses know if a man doesn't care for them."

The older man nodded, still idly stroking the nose of the horse.

"You're right there – animals know when someone means them well – or ill."

The younger man went to the foot of a nearby tree, and retrieved a battered bucket.

"There's some extra feed for him here – we don't have much, but I like to reward them for not kicking me away when I'm trying to sew them up."

They tethered the horse back on the end of the horse lines, far enough from the nearest other horse that he'd be able to eat in peace, and left him there. As they turned to walk back into the centre of the camp, the older man cleared his throat, as if he wanted to say something, and wasn't sure how the younger man would react. Eventually, he must have decided just to speak.

"Like I said, you do a good job of it. I dare say that you sew better than a lot of genteel young ladies do. I... I wasn't just passing today – I sought you out intentionally."

The younger man paused, startled.

"Intentionally? Whatever for? I haven't done anything to get me in trouble with the General, have I?"

The older man laughed, shaking his head.

"Far from it. Word has spread that you're good at putting the broken back together, and in the aftermath of battles, that's a very valuable skill. A skill I need. I'm a surgeon – the only one this regiment has, at present. I want to co-opt you to the medical corps – what there is left of it. I'm convinced that you'll be just as good at putting men back together as horses. In a way, men are easier – you can explain things to them, and they'll usually at least try to co-operate."

The last of the light was fading from the sky as they reached the cook tents, and they joined the queue in silence. It was only once they'd eaten that the younger man sighed, then gave a nod.

"I'll do it. You'll have much to teach me, for it's not a thing I ever thought to find myself doing, nor a thing I was raised for, but I'd far rather heal men than fight them."

The older man clapped him on the back.

"Good – no time to waste then – let me show you the hospital tent, and get you officially transferred to my company."

Chapter One

1817 – Early June in the English Countryside

"Eeeeeee!"

A piercing scream rent the air, shattering the peaceful warmth of the early June afternoon. The scream was followed by a dull 'thud', and Lady Venetia Chater thought, as she drifted in and out of the darkness, that someone must have fainted. But why? Why was everything black, why did her head hurt so much? Why…? She faded into unconsciousness, questions unanswered.

*****

Mr Morgan Follett had just left his horse with a rather distracted looking stable boy, and turned towards the main house at Brightwood Chase when the sound of a scream came to him on the summer air. A scream from the direction of the house. Concerned, he sprinted across the gravelled forecourt, and flung himself through the partly open door. Just inside, he near collided with a footman, who stood, stunned, staring at the scene before him.

A scene which, for a moment, took him back to places far from England.

He shook his head, trying to take it in. Two grooms held the ends of a makeshift stretcher, on which lay a woman. A woman whose head was covered in blood.

To one side, a maid lay crumpled on the floor, having apparently fainted, and a white-faced older woman bent over her, trying to rouse her. The man he assumed to be the butler stood not far from Morgan, trying, it seemed, to deal with the chaos.

They were all useless.

Morgan pushed past them, and went to the stretcher, bending down to look closely at the woman. There was certainly a lot of blood, but the cut was on her forehead, and not too deep – rather it was as if a section of her skin had been peeled back on one side of her brow, but not torn off completely. That was good – he could fix this – she would have a scar, of a certainty, but there was no threat of death, so long as infection was prevented.

He stood again, and took charge.

"Is there a parlour with good big windows and a large table? Large enough to set her upon, so that I can work on her forehead in good light? I'll also need basins of boiled water, clean – and I mean utterly clean – cloths, and the sewing basket of a Lady – this woman's, or another, it doesn't matter, so long as it contains good quality fine needles and thread. Oh, and laudanum, plus a tincture of Thyme if you have it. If not, a strong lye soap will do."

The staff stood in stunned silence for a moment, then the butler, apparently deciding that following the instructions of someone who seemed to know what they were doing was better than standing there, doing nothing, waved at the others, then spoke.

"Follow me – we will go to the grand parlour. Mrs Jenkins, please arrange the water, cloths, soap, laudanum and the like, and send a maid to gather one of the sewing boxes. You'd best send someone to inform her Ladyship, too."

That said, he walked past Morgan, speaking as he did.

"This way."

Morgan followed, and the two grooms brought the stretcher carefully. As they entered the parlour, the woman's eyes fluttered open for a moment, and settled on Morgan's face. They were a deep green shade, like leaves in the midst of summer, although clouded by confusion now. He felt an odd connection then, to this woman he had never seen before. But there was no time for such whimsy – her hurts needed to be dealt with.

They shifted her carefully onto the stout polished oak table, which was blessedly fairly close to the large windows.

"Open the curtains wide please, but also bring me a good oil lamp."

A footman scurried off to do as he'd bid, and moments later the Housekeeper hurried in, followed by two maids and a footman, all carrying various items. Morgan pulled a smaller table over to stand beside the large one, and set out the basins and other tools upon it. The Housekeeper handed him a sewing box.

"Will this suit? It's mine, and has the best needles I can afford."

Morgan opened it, and drew out the small tin she pointed to, which contained a number of slips of fabric with needles piercing them for storage. He sighed in relief – they were, indeed, high quality, and fine enough. There was also fine linen thread – not silk, which might have been better, but linen would do.

"This will do admirably. The laudanum?" The Housekeeper produced a small, tightly stoppered bottle from her pockets. "Thank you. Please give her just a drop or two, on her lips, so that she swallows it."

He took off his coat – no time for propriety here – rolled up his sleeves, and washed his hands with the soap. Then, into the other basin of water, he dripped some of the tincture of Thyme, before soaking a clean cloth in it. Then he threaded a needle, and set it to one side, ready.

Cleaning her wound took some time, for if she was to have the smallest scar possible, every speck of dirt and earth needed to be removed.

Every so often, her eyes flickered open, but eventually the laudanum took effect, and she slipped into sleep. Partway through the cleaning process, an older woman came into the room, and he heard a gasp, and a sob. Then the Housekeeper's voice.

"Come my Lady, you don't need to watch – he's doing a grand job of it, and you can't help her by watching. I'll get you some tea in the small parlour, shall I?"

They went away, without him having even lifted his eyes to see them. He was far too focused on the woman he tended.

Once it was as clean as he could get it, he gently tugged the loose flap of skin back into place and began to sew.

There would be a scar – an almost leaf shaped scar – but he would make it as unobtrusive as he could. Tiny stitches would be required, keeping the skin as flat and smooth as possible as he went. Not that it would matter, he thought, with a sad twist to his lips – she was a woman of the upper classes – such women were expected to be perfect, and the *ton* would likely be cruel to her for any scar at all. But he would do his best for her, because he had discovered that he felt compelled to help, to heal if he could, whether that was people or animals.

The laudanum began to wear off as he finished, and her eyes opened again, looking up at him. He stopped, not wanting her to frown, or move at all. They stayed that way for some time – likely only seconds, or at most minutes, but it felt like forever – and then she dropped back into sleep. He made the last few stitches, and tied it off neatly. Then he set the needle aside, wiped the whole area gently with the thyme infused water, and sat back.

Only then did he realise that the room was full – the Butler, Housekeeper, maids, footmen, and grooms had all been there, watching him work, silent and respectful. Morgan rose, and went to an armchair which stood to one side. The Housekeeper came to stand before him.

"I don't know who you are, but today you have saved the daughter of the house, and we are grateful. What can we do for you?"

Morgan shook his head.

"I came to collect the horse for the Baron of Crosswood. I've the money here. I'd appreciate a cup of tea, but then I'll be on my way. I'd suggest moving her to her own bed, and give her small – only small, mind – amounts of laudanum over the next few days, to ease the pain as it heals. But make sure that she wakes, and talks to you regularly, for it seems her head was hit hard. Gently wash the wound frequently with a clean, soft cloth soaked in water with Thyme tincture in it, but don't cover it, or use any salves or the like. That way the final scar will be as small as possible. The stitches will need to be carefully removed in about two weeks' time, once it's well sealed."

He stood then, rolled his sleeves back down, took his coat from the chair where he'd left it, and retrieved the pouch of money, before putting the coat on. The butler smiled.

"I'll leave Mrs Jenkins to arrange moving my Lady, and Molly here can get you that tea. If you'll come with me, I'll show you to Lady Hardenwell, and you can give the money directly to her."

Morgan followed him from the room, and was led to a smaller parlour, where an older woman sat, twisting her fingers. She looked up when the Butler showed him in.

"Is she....?"

"Your daughter will be well, my Lady, although she will have a scar. I have made it as neat as I possibly could, but it is impossible to completely avoid. But I am here now to give you this - the money from Baron Crosswood. If you are happy with that, I'll collect the horse and be on my way back to Crosswood Hall."

He held out the pouch, and the Lady took it, not even bothering to glance at its contents before setting it aside.

"Thank you... I don't know what I would have done..."

"There is no need for thanks – I could not have left a Lady in distress like that. Now I'll go out to the stables and collect the horse, if you've someone who can show me which one it is?"

She nodded, and looked to the Butler.

"I'll arrange that, my Lady."

Morgan bowed, and the Butler led him away, first to the kitchens for that cup of tea – and the cake that Morgan was given with it – and then he summoned one of the grooms to show Morgan the horse.

In the stables, Morgan finally heard the explanation for how the young Lady had come to be carried in on a stretcher.

She was, it seemed, a crack rider, and prone to being a little rash. A groom had been following her, and seen her send her horse at a huge hedge, with a drop on the other side, and a narrow space between two trees. There had been nothing he could do – her horse had slipped slightly on the take-off, and they had gone crashing through the top of the hedge, down into the drop on the other side, and slid down the hill, narrowly missing the larger trees, but being cut and scraped by the smaller saplings along the way.

Morgan thought, on hearing it, that she was lucky to be alive.

"What condition is her horse in?"

He'd had to ask… he was incapable of potentially leaving an animal injured if he could help. The groom shook his head in wonderment.

"Scratched up, but not severely damaged – it's a miracle. He'll be bruised for weeks, but he'll recover."

Morgan was glad to hear it.

Half an hour later, he was on his way, riding his own horse, and leading the one that Lord Crosswell had purchased. He wondered, as he rode, what would become of the young woman he'd just stitched up – had her rashness cost her any chance of a good match, because now she was scarred? Could he have done any better job of it?

He doubted that – and it wasn't his to worry about anyway.

*****

There was something cool on her forehead – cool and wet. She frowned, an automatic response to her puzzlement, and then wished that she hadn't. Her head hurt – both in the 'aches like the very devil' way, and in the 'feels like a healing cut' way.

Cautiously, she opened her eyes.

With a squeak of shock, her mother dropped the wet cloth – which fell completely over Venetia's face. Moments later, it was snatched away.

"Oh! Venetia! I am so glad that you're finally awake!"

Confusion filled her, and she tried very hard to remember why her head hurt, and why her mother might look so relieved. What had happened? What had she done, to end up in bed like this? Because she was utterly, completely certain that it was the result of something she had done – anything bad usually was.

Her memory remained blank. There were misty glimpses of a man's face, slightly tensed in concentration, and the sense of warmth in those deep brown eyes – but she didn't know if the man was real, or a dream. He certainly wasn't anyone she'd ever met. Beyond that, only blackness. There was nothing for it then, she'd have to ask.

"Mother... why am I like this? Why does my head hurt?"

Her mother's mouth formed a shocked 'O'.

"You don't remember?"

"No.... If I did, I wouldn't need to ask."

Her mother sighed.

"From the description the groom gave me, you were, as usual, entirely rash. You sent your horse at the big hedge amongst the copse of trees – the one with the drop into a ditch on the other side. The ground was a little wet, and your horse slipped on take-off. You went through the hedge, and the smaller trees. It's a wonder that your head wasn't broken open on one of the bigger ones."

Venetia took that in, thinking hard, trying to remember.

But little came to her beyond a blurry image of trees rushing past, and pain followed by darkness. Then something important occurred to her.

"My horse...? Is he...?"

"By some miracle he also survived – bruised and scratched, with sprained muscles I am told, but nothing worse."

A wash of relief filled her.

Cautiously, she lifted her hand to her forehead, where the stinging pain seemed more intense by the minute. Her fingertips met a pattern of ridges, and little bumps at the ends, with tiny tails of thread. Icy cold horror slid through her veins. There was no possibility that this could end in any way but with her having a very noticeable scar on her face.

"My face...?"

"Was a gory bloody mess, if you'll excuse me being blunt. One of the maids fainted and I very nearly did so when I saw it. Yes, you'll have a scar, but you're lucky that it's not far worse."

"How... why...?"

Her mother laughed then, a bitter, sad sound.

"How does your face come to be stitched up like this?"

"Yes – there's no surgeon within a day's travel..."

"I can only say that you were granted a miracle. A man had just arrived to collect the horse we sold to Lord Crosswood. He got here just as the grooms carried you in on the stretcher. I was upstairs, and the staff were all struck by horror and fear. He walked in, took one look, knew exactly what to do, issued orders, and did what was needed when Mrs Jenkins provided everything he asked for. When I came down, he was already cleaning your face and preparing to stitch it up. What could I do but let him continue? Without help, you would just as likely have died, from blood loss or infection and, even if you'd lived, you would have had the most horrific scar."

She shuddered and Venetia wondered just how bad it had been.

"And this is not 'the most horrific scar'?"

"No, it is not. Far from it. The stitches are tiny, delicate, better than all but the best embroidery. He spent a very long time trying his best to disfigure you as little as possible. But one cannot repair a gaping wound without some stitches, so there will be a scar. It will be dark to begin with, but like all scars, it will fade with time, and become less obvious."

Venetia absorbed her words, trying hard to accept that she would be scarred for the rest of her life. It was a most difficult concept to accept – especially as there was no one to blame but herself.

"Then... we won't be going to London in the Autumn, won't be attending Balls and Soirees? Because surely a scar will make people turn away from me, especially when it is still relatively new, and dark in colour?"

Her mother took a deep breath, and shook her head sadly.

"Venetia... we have no choice. We will wait until late September, to give it some time, but we will still go, and you will still do your best to make a match. The money we have will not last much past Christmas, although I have still managed to keep aside a small dowry for you. Last year's harvest was bad, and this year's looks only a little better. And that is all we have – the harvest from this estate. Your uncle may have inherited your father's title, but the man feels no compulsion to assist us at all."

Venetia felt the pain in her head acutely, her mother's words crushing all of her hopes for the future. There would be no charming younger man for her now – only the old men in search of a young wife would accept a woman with a scarred face – the men who cared more for a woman's body than her face...

A sob broke free, despite her attempts to stop it.

"But... they will mock me, I am sure..."

"Then you will be strong, and ignore them, and show the quality of your character. Now rest – I will send for some tea, and with that, you can have a few drops of laudanum, to help you sleep and heal. In a few days' time, it should begin to not hurt so much."

Venetia nodded, but that hurt too, and a small laugh escaped her, full of near hysterical bitterness.

"I promise, Mother, that in future, when you tell me not to be so wild and rash, I will actually listen."

Her mother pulled the bellpull, then turned back to her with a true smile.

"I know that you mean that now, but I do not, for one minute, believe that intention will last. Being a little wild is simply part of you, my dear daughter, and I do not think I would like a totally sedate and obedient version of you, no matter how much trouble that might save me."

Chapter Two

Despite their best efforts, Venetia spent close to a week in bed, being slightly feverish. The cut healed, but it was a little swollen, and tender to the touch, even though her mother and Mrs Jenkins had precisely followed the man's instructions, and kept it perfectly clean. Finally, there came the day when Venetia woke to feeling clear of head and less aching of body, and with the desire to eat. She assumed that meant that she was actually getting better.

One thing that had not improved, however, was her memory of the day of her fall. The little she did remember was blurry and confusing – a mixture of darkness, pain, falling, and a man's face. A man with deep brown eyes that were like forest pools – deep enough to drown in. A man she wasn't certain was real. Her mother, Mrs Jenkins, and the maids had all told her their versions of what had happened, and none of it made sense.

How could a man who was dressed as a groom, and had come to collect a horse, have the skill and knowledge to perform the work of a surgeon – and perform it well, as they said? But they all agreed on the point that he had come to collect the horse, and on the point of his standard of dress.

Her stomach rumbled, and she pushed away thoughts of the man, focusing on reaching the small bell which lay on her bedside table, so that she could ring for breakfast.

Later that day, she rose from her bed for the first time since the fall, and was shocked at how weak and unstable she felt. She had wanted to go to the stables, to see how well her horse had recovered, but getting downstairs to the parlour proved to be nearly beyond her – the stables would have to wait for another day.

"Why are you looking so blue-devilled, Venetia? You should be happy that you're well enough to be sitting down here, drinking tea in the parlour!"

She sighed.

"I know, Mother. But... I don't like feeling weak, and I especially don't like not being able to remember any of the last week, or more, clearly!"

"I, and all of the staff, have told you everything that we saw, everything that we know about what happened – what more do you need? What worries you so much?"

Venetia set the tea cup down, her hand only shaking slightly.

"I don't know, really. I'd like to remember exactly what happened. But that's not what worries me most. I'd like to know more about the man whose stitchery now graces my forehead. We don't even know his name! I would thank him, if I could – I may now be scarred for life, but I am sensible of the fact that it could have been far worse, without his intervention."

"That is kind of you – and honourable – but really, there is nothing we can do. It's best that you put those thoughts aside, and concentrate on healing, and preparing for our time in London – mentally and physically. After all, it is almost certain that we will never see that man again."

*****

Morgan took his time riding back to Crosswood, even though that meant staying overnight in an Inn along the way – the hours of working on the girl's face had taken a heavy toll.

Lord Crosswood would not be worried – he trusted that Morgan would do things at a pace which was best for himself, and the horse. Having seen the horses settled in the Inn stables he ate an early dinner and went up to bed. The room was small, but clean and comfortable, for which he was grateful, and the maid came and lit a small fire as, even in summer, the nights could be cool.

He sat in the chair beside the hearth, planning to read a little before sleeping, only to find himself waking, still in the chair, hours later. That sleep had been shallow, drifting, full of dreams – dreams in which he saw the girl's bloodied face again, dreams in which he imagined seeing her take that jump, and fall, dreams in which her leaf green eyes met his, full of some inexplicable meaning.

It had not been restful.

He shook his head, picked his book up from where it had fallen, then rose and stretched. Time to actually go to bed, and hopefully sleep far better. Tomorrow would be a miserable day on the road if he got no true rest.

Once in bed, he dropped almost immediately into sleep – sleep which was again filled with green eyes and a sense of unexplained importance. Still, he slept well enough to wake feeling refreshed with the dawn. Perhaps her face would stop haunting him once he got home.

By midday, he was nearing Crosswood, and his thoughts were mostly upon the tasks that awaited him there – the care of Lord Crosswood's horses, the plans for next year's breeding season, and the selection of the next horses to buy. He shook his head, bemused at what his life had become. The son of a second son, his claim to noble blood did not bring him anything of significance – he had, as expected of a man of that birth, gone into the military, which had suited him only barely better than the church would have, but he had not, ever, thought to end up working as a stablemaster.

Many would say it was beneath him, yet he found pleasure in it, for horses were far less demanding than men, and far more appreciative of care.

He gave a snort of laughter at the thought, as he rode up the long drive to Crosswood Hall. Beneath him... he was quite sure that the young Lady whose face he had sewn up regarded grooms and stable men of all kinds as beneath her, yet his skills had saved her from the worst consequences of her rashness.

What would she think about him, if she ever saw him again? Not that she would, of course – he had no reason to move in such circles as she would spend her life in. He had no need of high society, no need of anything but the life he had now, which was peaceful, satisfying, and generally without drama.

*****

A week after his return to Crosswood, Morgan was in the stables, where the last expected foal of the year had just been born. There was something delightful about new foals, with their gangly legs and curious nature, which restored his faith in the world. The mare nuzzled the foal, and Morgan had just managed to get it up and balanced on its legs to drink from its mother, when a sound came behind him.

"Excuse me, Mr Follett."

Morgan slipped out of the loosebox into the stable corridor, and found a footman waiting for him.

"Yes?"

"Lord Crosswood asks that you come to his study. He said to tell you that it is regarding an important matter."

Morgan raised his eyebrows, curious, but not immediately worried. He got on well with his employer, who had always been a most reasonable man. He looked down at himself with a wry grin.

"I'd best go and clean up a little then – the birthing of foals is a messy business. Please let Lord Crosswood know that I will be there as soon as I'm presentable."

"Certainly."

The footman turned and went back towards the house, leaving Morgan to wash his hands and face in the nearby trough before he hurried up the stairs to his quarters above the carriage house. Fifteen minutes later, scrubbed and dressed in clean clothes, Morgan quickly looked in on the mare and foal, and then set off across the stable forecourt to the back door of Crosswood Hall.

Lord Crosswood's study was on the ground floor, at the back of the house – a position well suited to meeting with his estate manager or his staff, as well as merchants who came to sell their produce to the estate. It reminded Morgan of his own father's small study – full of books, ledgers, stacks of papers and the like.

He tapped on the door, and Lord Crosswood bid him enter.

"You wanted to see me, my Lord? I apologise for the delay, but Mist has just delivered a healthy filly, and I was... not in a clean enough state to come into the house – I had to change."

Lord Crosswood nodded, smiling, and waved Morgan to a chair.

"A filly, you say? That's good – more breeding stock. Let's hope that she'll be as well put together as her mother, eh?"

"Indeed, my Lord."

Lord Crosswood looked almost nervous, and Morgan wondered just what this was about – but it wasn't his place to ask. If the Lord wanted to speak to him about something, he'd get to it in his own time.

So he allowed the silence to stretch.

Lord Crosswood tapped his fingers on the desk for a moment, then reached out to one side where two letters lay, one sealed, one with the seal broken. He lifted the sealed one, and pushed it across the desk to Morgan. Morgan glanced at it, puzzled, and found that it was addressed to him.

"This came today, enclosed in a covering letter to me. Before I say anything more, before we have the conversations which this will require, I will leave you to read it."

That statement sent a shiver down Morgan's spine – what on Earth could be in that letter?

He did not recognise the seal, or the hand it was addressed in, neither of which facts gave any reassurance at all. He took a deep breath, lifted the missive, then broke the seal.

He read it, and then, shaking his head in disbelief, read it again. The words stayed the same.

He felt, in that moment, detached from everything, as if the world was not real. For what was on those pages changed everything, upending his life utterly, all in an instant. He looked up at Lord Crosswell, sure that his face had gone pale.

"I... I don't know what..."

Lord Crosswell nodded.

"Take your time about it, let it sink in. I offer you both my condolences, and my congratulations. I have just one request of you, before your new life sweeps you away – can you please find me a new stablemaster who is even half as good as you are?"

*****

Mid-August 1817

As soon as she heard the click of the front door closing, Venetia set aside her book, and hurried out of the parlour to intercept her mother. From Lady Hardenwell's expression, the meeting with their man of business had not gone entirely well.

"Mother?"

Lady Hardenwell sighed.

"Let us go back into the parlour. I will send for some tea, and then I'll tell you about it."

Venetia was glad, for the thousandth time, that her mother was a competent woman, who thought that her daughter should also be regarded as intelligent and competent. It meant that Venetia was told everything about their finances, and the workings of the estate, rather than being 'protected' from such things, as so many young women were.

They settled onto their favourite chairs, and said nothing at all until the tea tray had been delivered, and the maid had left the room. For a moment after that, they sipped tea, and appreciated the flavour. Then Lady Hardenwell set her cup down.

"It is not entirely good, but also not entirely bad. This year's harvest has been far better than the last two years' harvests, but still not as good as we had hoped for. And costs have risen, so we are not quite breaking even. The reserve funds we had are nearly exhausted. We will have enough to get to Christmastide, and maybe a little beyond, but we will need to sell at least one more horse, and one of the carriages."

Venetia felt a little ill at her mother's words – she had hoped that the harvest would save them, at least until next year.

"Then...?"

"We will have to go to London, four weeks from now, and you must do your very best to make a match with a respectable and wealthy man, who is of the kind of character which will lead him to assisting his wife's mother...."

Venetia's hand went to her forehead, without any conscious intent on her part, and a small sob escaped her lips.

"But... this is so obvious – it looks as if a small autumn leaf has stuck to my face! The scar is still so dark, so very noticeable – I am sure that I will be mocked by the ladies, and disregarded by the gentlemen, because I am so clearly not perfect!"

Her mother, quite shockingly, made no attempt to deny the truth of her words. Venetia wanted, then, to cast herself down on the couch and cry – yet she knew that would not help in the least. Instead, she swallowed the tears, lifted her teacup, and sipped, forcing herself to be calm.

After a long silence, Lady Hardenwell gave a slow nod.

"You are right. Yet that changes nothing. A good marriage for you is the key to our survival, going forward. We will go to London, and you will, at the very least, try. We can arrange your hair so that some curls fall over that side of your forehead, and we can apply some face powder to minimise the colour of the scar. I am sure that, once a gentleman gets past the initial visual surprise, and actually talks to you, it will all go well."

Venetia shook her head.

"You have more faith in the gentlemen of the *ton* than I have, Mother. But if it is our only option, then, certainly, I will try."

But I hold little hope...

Chapter Three

Early September 1817

"What do you think, Mother? Will the gossips speak badly of me for moving to half mourning? Personally, I am glad to move on from wearing unrelieved black."

"They can say what they like – I doubt that it will be any more than the muttering that already exists. And, after all, he was your uncle, not your father – I think that three months of full mourning is quite enough. You need to be out and about in society, to be seen, to be becoming known, to be making alliances. A few months in London at this time of year will achieve much of that, and be much easier than waiting until Spring, and the full whirl of the Season."

He gave a soft laugh, and shook his head.

"I don't think that any part of this will be easy – any more than the last three months have been! But I have no choice, do I? I never expected to come into the title – Father dying young was distressing, but changed nothing, as far as my position in the world. I could not, however, have predicted that my uncle, his wife, and all three of his children would be taken off by the cholera, within days of each other."

"You are doing admirably, never fear. I'm proud of you, and I'm sure that society will come to respect you. You don't lack for courage, and you're far more sensible than most of them are. So long as you go about things cautiously, all will be well. But you will need to think about marrying, to ensure that there is an heir – and that means that you will be very popular... with the matchmaking mothers."

He groaned.

"That, I do not look forward to at all. I am not against marriage, of a certainty, but I will marry when I am ready, to a woman of my choice, a woman I can care for, and respect as a person. I have no interest in a marriage where affection is not part of it. I am glad that you raised me with an understanding of how society goes about things, even if we never expected me to need to move in those circles, but that just confirms to me that I do not wish to become like them, even if I am now technically of that status."

"You will do as you wish, and I know that you will also do your best for the Earldom – you have already repaired some of your uncle's unwise practices, and the estates are thriving. For the next two weeks, before we go to London, I will do my best to give you as much information as possible about who has influence, and who to be wary of. There are advantages to the fact that I am a Duke's daughter, and those who mocked me for marrying a second son – 'beneath me' they said – will likely see things differently, now that you are Earl of Templewick."

"Thank you, Mother. You cannot know how grateful I am for your help."

*****

Venetia stared out of the carriage window as they passed through the streets of London. She kept the hood of her cloak pulled up around her face, for warmth, and to hide the scar, but she could not resist watching the city pass by.

And, truthfully, she watched because doing so gave her something else to think about, beyond the coming weeks of going about in society, with her scarred face on view for all to see.

"We are nearly there, Venetia. Do sit back and prepare yourself. We have to make sure that we make a positive impression. At least your uncle has been generous enough to allow us to stay in Hardenwell House. I know that it is galling to have to stay as a guest in the house which was once ours, but it, like so much else, went to your uncle when your father died. And, as we are dependent on your uncle's charity in this matter, we must be nice to him, and to your cousin, even if you find the whole family less than appealing to be with."

Venetia sighed.

"Yes, Mother. I know – I will do my best. I haven't seen Cousin Jasper since we were both small children, so I've no idea what I will think of him – or he of me. Perhaps he is not too much like his father?"

"We can hope...."

They lapsed into silence, and a short while later, the carriage drew up outside Hardenwell House. A rush of childhood memories momentarily swamped Venetia, and she gave a little ragged gasp, sternly telling herself that this was no time to be maudlin. Her mother reached across and took her hand for a moment, before releasing her as a footman opened the door.

She stepped out, a small frown creasing her brow – she had never seen this footman before – had her uncle employed new staff? Or extra staff? When the house had transferred to him after her father's death, all of the staff had, as far as she knew, stayed on. Perhaps... some of them had left? That thought sent a small shiver down her spine, for the only thing she could think of which might have made those staff leave was if the new master of the house did not treat them well. She would see – perhaps there had just been extra staff added – but still, it seemed a bad omen.

At the door of the house, Ames, the butler, greeted them with a small smile. Venetia's concern eased a little – at least Ames was still here.

His eyes skimmed across her face, and she saw the moment when he noticed the scar, saw the tiny flinch, the widening of his eyes. This was how it was going to be, every time someone saw her for the first time – an eternity of people flinching from the sight of her. She sighed softly.

"Welcome, Lady Hardenwell, Lady Venetia. Your rooms have been prepared."

A small frown slipped across his face for a moment, rapidly banished, and replaced with his normal impassive 'professional' face. Beside her, Lady Hardenwell stiffened – it seemed that she had noticed that momentary frown too.

"Ames… which rooms have we been given?"

Her mother's voice was steady, but somehow, brittle… Ames swallowed, and Venetia was certain that he was uncomfortable.

"The green and the blue guest suites, my Lady."

Venetia bit her lip to prevent a shocked gasp escaping her. Those were the smallest of the guest suites, the ones which had not been refurbished for some years, and neither had a private sitting room attached. At least they each had a dressing room.

"I see. And where is our maid to be housed?"

"In… in the attic rooms, my Lady."

Lady Hardenwell drew herself up and spoke forcefully.

"That is, as I am sure you are aware, all entirely unsuitable. We must have our maid closer than that, and really, for Venetia to be suitably prepared to go out in society, we will need better rooms, with at least one private sitting room. Who decided that we should be placed in those rooms?"

This time, Ames actually looked embarrassed.

"Lord Hardenwell, my Lady."

In that instant, Venetia discovered that it was perfectly possible to dislike her uncle more than she already had.

"I see. Then I will have to take the matter up with him. Is he in residence?"

Ames shook his head.

"I'm sorry, my Lady, but no. And..." his voice dropped to a whisper, and he leant forward, "...I did attempt to advise on the inappropriateness... but my advice was... not accepted."

Her mother's lips formed a thin line.

"Thank you, Ames, for trying. Where is my brother-in-law, if not here, might I ask?"

"He and his wife have gone to Hard Abbey. I believe that they will be gone for a week, or perhaps two. Lord Jasper is still in residence, and currently in charge of the house."

The tone of Ames' voice made it clear that he disapproved of Lord Jasper, and especially of giving him any authority. At his words, however, Venetia saw an expression cross her mother's face – an expression which she knew all too well. It was the expression which indicated that her mother had a plan, and that the subject of that plan was, not to put too fine a point on it, doomed.

"Is he now? Well, I shall just have to speak to him about the matter, shan't I? Where might I find him now?"

Ames again, rather startlingly, allowed his feelings on the matter to appear on his face for a moment.

"Lord Jasper is still abed, my Lady – he was out rather late last night, as is his habit."

The glint in her mother's eye intensified.

"Then I must ask you to get his valet to rouse him. We – and our luggage – will wait in the parlour until he comes down. You can assure him that I will make quite the scene – even going as far as coming up and dragging him from his bed – if he doesn't have the courtesy to come down and speak to me appropriately. I will not have myself, or my daughter, treated so shabbily."

At that, there was a fleeting gleam in Ames' eyes which thoroughly matched the one that had been in her mother's, moments before. He bowed.

"Of course, my Lady. I'll have some tea sent in to you, while you wait."

With that, he turned and went, directing a footman to show them to the parlour – not that they needed to be shown the way, it was simply the principle of the thing, the carrying out of proper behaviour.

The parlour had barely changed – there were some different paintings on the wall, and a new carpet on the floor, but otherwise it was just the same. Another wave of memories assaulted Venetia, and she pushed those thoughts aside. They settled on the couch, and two footmen carried in their trunks behind them.

"Where should we put these, and the rest, my Lady?"

"Here, for now – once I resolve the matter of our rooms, I will ring for you."

She pointed to the corner of the room, and they, after exchanging a glance and shrug, set the trunks down, and went back out to collect the rest from the carriage. Not long after, a maid came in with a tea tray – a maid that they recognised, thankfully.

"Just set it down here, thank you Rosie."

The maid did so, eyeing the luggage, then, with an almost conspiratorial grin, she curtsied and slipped back out of the room. Venetia was beginning to suspect that the staff did not like her cousin, at all.

The tea was excellent, and the lemon biscuits that accompanied it were a delight – a delight which Venetia thought indicated that the Cook had also stayed on. She indulged in eating too many of them while they waited. A wait which extended, and extended. She turned to her mother.

"Perhaps you're going to have to follow through on your threat..."

That was the moment, of course, that the door opened to admit Lord Jasper Chater. They rose.

He resembled his father, and, to some extent, Venetia's own father, reminding Venetia of a painting she'd seen of her father as a young man. His dark hair was in mild disarray – intentionally, she thought – but his attire was immaculate. He must have a very good valet. His expression on seeing them, and the pile of luggage in the corner, was telling. He looked utterly annoyed, and then, as his eyes came to rest on Venetia's face, on her scar to be precise, a sneer twisted his lips. He bowed, rather mockingly.

Venetia's stomach clenched.

"Good day to you Aunt, Cousin. What is so very important that you had to insist on dragging me from my well-earned rest? And why on earth is the parlour cluttered up with your luggage? Why hasn't it been taken to your rooms?"

"Jasper. I see that your manners have not improved since your childhood. But that aside, the reason I asked for your presence is the same reason that our trunks are here. The rooms which we have been allocated are inadequate to our needs. I lived in this house for twenty years – do you not think that I recognise it when I am being offered the worst suites in the building? You will, thank you, immediately change that allocation to better rooms, ones close to each other with at least one private sitting room, and a small room attached for our maid."

Jasper spluttered, shocked at being so addressed by a woman. If I remembered aright, his mother had always spoiled him.

"I do not see that you are in a position to make demands, Aunt."

"Simply the fact that I am your aunt entitles me to be treated with appropriate courtesy and consideration. We are here to introduce Venetia to society, now that our mourning is over – we require rooms which will allow us to do that effectively, and in comfort. This house is large – you have no need to relegate us to the smallest rooms – the only reason which I can see for doing so is spite. And spite is a remarkably unbecoming thing in a gentleman."

Jasper looked rather as if he might explode, either from outright anger, or perhaps simply from being challenged.

His eyes narrowed, and he turned his sharp gaze directly upon Venetia.

"Introducing her to society? Whatever are you thinking, Aunt? She is, quite clearly, disfigured. Her form is pleasant, I'll give you that, but no man is going to want a woman with a disfigured face – unless, of course, she comes with a substantial dowry?" He paused, waiting for a few seconds, then laughed nastily. "No? I didn't think so. Perhaps she should resign herself to being some man's mistress, unless she wants the life of a shrivelled old spinster?"

Her breath left her. It was if she had fallen from a horse, landing in that way which resembles a fist to the stomach, and steals breath in a blaze of pain. Such cruelty in his words! She turned her eyes to her mother, to see Lady Hardenwell standing calmly, her shoulders tensed and her eyes hard.

"It is not up to you to judge so. Not all men are as narrow-minded and mean-spirited as you apparently are. And do not think that I am unaware of your behaviour, and... reputation. I will, for now, pretend that your inappropriate and unpleasant words were never spoken. But I will not forget. And if you do not at least behave with basic civility, I do believe that some of that behaviour may be noticed by the gossips of the *ton*. Which would be unfortunate, would it not? Especially if they should learn of the scale of your debts? I would suggest that you direct the staff to prepare the burgundy suite, and the gold suite with the adjoining sitting room, and the attached maid's rooms. That will allow us to remove ourselves and our luggage from your presence. We will be quite happy to be as inconspicuous as possible, once we are in those rooms – we would not want to disturb your daily... activities."

Jasper had been getting redder in the face by the moment, until Lady Hardenwell got to the part about his debts – how her mother knew of them, she could not imagine, but she was glad that such information was to hand, as Jasper's face lost all colour at those words. His debts, Venetia surmised, must be of truly terrifying proportions – and perhaps those debts were not known to his parents?

He stood there as she finished speaking, his face twisted, obviously fighting an internal battle.

Then, he gave another sharp, mocking bow.

"I see that you have the advantage of me, for now, Aunt. But I will not forget either. I will direct the staff as you suggest, and I will, most definitely, appreciate it if you do remain inconspicuous."

He turned on his heel and left the room.

Venetia and her mother collapsed onto the couch again, and it was only then that Venetia realised that her mother was shaking. She reached out, refilled her mother's tea cup, and handed it to her.

"That, Mother, was most courageous of you."

Her mother laughed.

"That was pure outrage speaking. I let my anger carry me, so that I did not think too closely of what I was doing – after all, he could as easily have chosen to throw us out. I... I don't actually have information on his debts – that was a guess – but I took one look and was sure that he'd have some, and that he'd have kept them from his father. Now I'll have to discover the details, in case I actually need to use them."

Venetia laughed, startled and delighted, nearly spilling her tea.

"And you berate me for being rash and taking risks! I think, Mother, that I now know where I got that trait from..."

*****

"Good evening, Lord Templewick. It is so good to see you again, even though still being in half-mourning no doubt limits your social activities somewhat. Might I introduce my daughter?"

He bowed, his eyes flicking to the young Lady who waited behind the woman who'd spoken – Lady Horsham, he thought – with a demure expression. He would allow an introduction, as he did for all of them, and be kind to her, without giving any indication of being interested in her. It was only polite to do so.

"Of course, Lady Horsham – and thank you for your consideration with respect to my mourning."

Lady Horsham nodded, and waved her daughter forward.

"Lord Templewick, this is my eldest daughter, Lady Petrina Bellwood. Petrina, please be known to the Earl of Templewick."

He bowed over the girl's hand, watching a blush stain her cheeks. She was plumper than was fashionable, and her skin was that unfortunate shade which went instantly blotchy when she blushed. She was quite obviously aware of what would be perceived, amongst the *ton*, as her shortcomings, and looked embarrassed.

"Lady Petrina – I am delighted to meet you. Are you having a pleasant evening?"

She took a deep breath, as if steeling herself for something.

"I... I am, Th.. Th.. Thank you, Lord Templewick."

The slight stutter explained the embarrassment. The poor girl – it was the sort of imperfection which would be judged harshly by the *ton*. He chose, therefore, to ignore it. He knew full-well that imperfections did not make horses, or people, incapable – far from it – it was often those with such challenges who were the most talented in various ways.

They spoke for another few minutes, and her stutter eased as she realised that he would not mock her, and that he was genuinely interested in what she had to say. He hoped, for her sake, that she would find a man who could see past the stutter to the person. From the sound of it, her life was rather dull, and the need to find a husband a terrible trial to her. She did not have the sort of personality which appealed to him, but he would not simply cruelly push her aside – he suspected that all too many men had already done that, as soon as they had heard her speak.

By the end of the evening, he had been introduced to many young women – and had concluded that the next few months were going to be even more painful than he had originally thought.

Chapter Four

They had been in London for three days now, and, so far, they had barely seen Lord Jasper – he was out late every night, did not eat dinner at home, and was generally too busy with his own entertainments to bother with them – which suited Venetia and her mother perfectly. They had been to the modiste's, and the milliner's, and Venetia felt as if she had pin holes all over her from the measuring and fitting. The milliner had assured her that she could create bonnets and head pieces which would partly hide the scar – which made her feel a little better about it all.

Still, everywhere they went, people noticed the scar, and stared. If this was how people reacted on the street, how much worse was it going to be at a ball, amidst the cream of society?

If it had not been for the scar, that terrible branding which reminded her at every moment of her own rash foolishness, she would have enjoyed herself – for the gowns she was to have were beautiful, and she had always loved dancing... But she had also always wanted others to find her attractive, to be pleasant to her.

She lay in her bed, tired, but unable to sleep, remembering, over and over, the expressions on people's faces, during the day, as they had noticed her scar. It was a waking nightmare.

Eventually, she rose, pulled a robe around her, and slipped out of the room. She would go down to the kitchen and find some small thing to eat, and perhaps something to drink. She had always done that, as a child, and Cook had left a little tray out for her, just in case. She smiled at the thought.

The house was dark and still – in the darkness, she could almost pretend that it was still theirs, that her father still lived, and that all was well – almost. In the kitchen, she went to the sideboard where all of the pots were lined up, ready for the morning, and there, just as it had been years ago, was a small tray, with a glass of sugared lemon water, some bread, some cheese, and some sausage.

At the sight, tears welled in her eyes, and she stopped before touching it, that potent symbol which told her that someone other than her mother still cared for her. It took some moments, but she regained her composure, and took the tray to the kitchen table, to sit and eat. When she was finished, she set the tray back where she had found it, and turned to go back to her room.

As she stepped into the corridor, the back servant's door to the house opened, and Lord Jasper, obviously thoroughly in his cups, stumbled through. He turned, fumbling, and locked the door. It must, Venetia realised, have been left open specifically for him. She froze where she was for a moment, then cautiously tried to slip back into the kitchen, silently.

She must have made some sound, however, for Lord Jasper turned sharply, his eyes searching his surroundings until they lit upon her. A strange smile crossed his face then – it was harsh, almost predatory. The silence extended – she did not know what to do – her first instinct was to flee, but he was between her and the stairs. She took a step back, finding herself against the doorframe, as if the threat of him had pushed her. That movement seemed to free him from whatever had held him still, and with two long strides he was close in front of her.

His arms shot out, going one either side of her, trapping her against the edge of the door as he leered at her.

His voice, when it came, was low, a little rough from drink.

"Well now, what have we here? A wanton, barely clothed, wandering the halls in the deep of night – something that no decent woman would do. If you're going to behave like the cheapest of lightskirts, I can only see that as an invitation – one I am happy to accept. After all, with that scar, you should get used to being grateful for any attention a man might deign to give you."

The words shocked her, pinning her in place as surely as his arms did, but then he laughed softly, and the growing chill of fear inside her was replaced by fury. She would not accept this as her fate!

He bent his head, moving his body hard against her, his lips seeking hers. The stench of the spirits he'd consumed accosted her senses, and she nearly gagged. Then, triggered by that, the fury drove her and, rash as always, thinking of nothing but escaping the situation, of punishing him for his arrogant, demeaning presumption, she twisted at the last moment, forcing his lips to her cheek rather than her mouth, and lifted her knee forcefully, ensuring its firm collision with his most private parts.

"Ooomph." Barely able to speak at that moment, he staggered back, his arms dropping to clutch at his injured parts, thus freeing her. She spun and ran. His voice followed her up the stairs. "Ungrateful slattern! You'll pay for this, I swear!"

Venetia didn't stop running until she was in her rooms, with the door barred behind her. Then she flung herself down onto the bed and cried – tears of anger, frustration and more. She wished, desperately, that she had never taken that jump, had never put herself in the situation which had resulted in the scar. But she had, and nothing would ever be the same again.

And for the next few months, she had to live in this house – this house which was full of her memories, and which was now occupied by Lord Jasper. She did not doubt his paucity of character, nor the fact that he would, after tonight, be attempting to trap her at any opportunity. It was just another thing which would make her life miserable, just another thing which brought home to her how hopeless their situation was.

*****

As he had done so often since that June day, Morgan woke from a dream where he was sewing up an injury on a girl's face. In the dream, it took forever, never being completed, and he woke exhausted, certain that he had done a terrible job. He sat up in bed, staring at the rather opulent room around him. So much had changed since June...

Had he done a good enough job? Was the young woman horribly scarred? He would likely never know, for he did not know her name. He knew of her mother simply as Lady Hardenwell, a widow – but he'd had no indication of her actual title – she might have been the widow of a Duke, or of a Baronet, each as easily as the other. It hadn't seemed important to know, at the time – but now, everything was different. He might, as likely as not, meet the mother and daughter out in society – if, that was, he had done a neat enough job on her face for her to be venturing out in society at all.

What if he had not? If he had not been able to save her ability to be seen in society, he would feel guilty, no matter that her fall was no fault of his.

He shook the thoughts aside, rang for his valet – and that was still a strange concept, indeed – and rose. He had a great deal to do, today as every day since he had received that fateful letter, informing him of his uncle's, aunt's, and cousins' deaths. The responsibilities of the title weighed on him, as did the fact that his uncle had not been the best of managers, and had left his estate in less than perfect condition. But Morgan was not one to shirk. He accepted the challenges, and faced them with determination, even though, much of the time, he wished himself back in the simple life of a stablemaster.

Today, he would spend hours with the new estate manager he had employed, and with the family man of business, reviewing his investments and the plans for the coming year's crops. He prayed that the crops would do better than those of this year, and last year, for the weather had been dreadful, and the harvests poor.

He was staring out of the window, contemplating all that faced him, when his valet slipped into the room.

"I have meetings this morning with the man of business and the estate manager. Please dress me as you see to be appropriate, if you would, Mullard."

"Of course, my Lord."

Mullard bowed, and went into the dressing room, returning shortly with clothing which he laid out on the bed. Morgan submitted to the strange process of having someone else dress him, his mind going back to the day ahead, and all that must be done.

Tonight, he was to attend a Ball. He did not, he had concluded, like society events at all, but attending them was necessary, as was being a member of White's, and socialising with gentlemen there. Without the connections that such things brought, he would not have access to good investment opportunities, nor, when the time came, to a woman suitable for an advantageous marriage.

That thought made him shudder, causing his valet to make a tiny, exasperated noise as the movement made his hand slip while adjusting Morgan's cravat.

"My apologies, Mullard. Eventually I'll get used to this, and manage to make it easier for you."

The valet waved a hand.

"I'm sure you will, my Lord. In truth, it's a pleasure to dress you, for you've a good figure on you, and look well in your clothes – unlike many a gentleman I've worked for in the past."

Morgan smiled, then stilled himself again as Mullard went back to work on the cravat. The end result was remarkable – a knot that Morgan could not have tied himself, ever. He studied himself in the mirror, and concluded that, overall, Mullard was right – he looked good in quality clothes. It was something he was grateful for, as it gave him more confidence when walking into a room full of the *ton*, beneath the eagle eyes of the gossips who controlled the social status of one and all.

But that consideration brought his thoughts back to the fact that he would be expected to marry one of the young ladies who were found at such events, and to do so relatively soon. As an unmarried Earl who was reasonably young, healthy, and quite good looking, he was automatically a target for those women seeking a good match.

It rather amused him that not one of them would have looked at him twice, just three months ago...

*****

Venetia shivered, not because the evening was cold, but because she was three steps away from being greeted by the hosts of the Ball. Three steps away from seeing 'that look' on their faces, as they took note of her scar. It was a look she had already seen on the faces of the people either side of them in the receiving line, on the faces of people who had passed her in the street when she went out with her mother – on the faces of every person who saw her.

She dreaded it more with every passing day.

And tonight, at her first Ball, she would discover whether she would be shunned completely or not.

If she was lucky, perhaps a gentleman would take pity upon her, and dance with her – but she doubted that. Still, her mother knew many ladies, even if she had not seen them for some years, so perhaps there was some hope of her at least being included in conversation.

The people before them stepped away and, all too soon, they stood before their hosts, Lord and Lady Cotteridge. Her mother spoke, even as Lady Cotteridge's eyes traversed Venetia's face.

"Thank you for the invitation, my Lord, my Lady – might I present my daughter, Lady Venetia Chater?"

Venetia curtsied.

As she rose, her eyes went to Lord Cotteridge's face, where an expression of distaste had appeared, then she looked again at Lady Cotteridge, whose expression was one of pity. The Lady spoke.

"I am delighted to meet you, Lady Venetia. I knew your mother when we both first came out into society – it is good to see her again."

Lord Cotteridge gave a rather insincere smile.

"Delighted to see you again, Lady Hardenwell, and to meet you, Lady Venetia."

He didn't sound in the least delighted.

They moved on, towards the ballroom, as the next in line stepped up to greet the hosts.

At the top of the steps which led down into the large room, an usher stood, announcing the new arrivals. Each announcement caused a momentary lapse in conversation in the room as those present turned to observe the new arrivals. This time, as the eyes of all of those people took in Venetia, that pause lasted longer than the previous ones, and then, when conversation resumed, it resumed as a wave of whispers, flowing out across the room from where they stood.

It was excruciating, and it took every scrap of courage she had not to just turn and run from the building. Her mother gripped her arm, and squeezed it gently, then led her down the steps, her head held high.

Venetia tried to emulate her mother's confident manner, but she was quite sure that she had gone dreadfully pale. People whispered behind fans as they passed, and Venetia saw a number of gentlemen turn away with expressions which clearly indicated that they found the sight of her face repugnant. There was nothing she could do but ignore it, and allow her mother to lead her – wherever they might be going.

Which turned out to be a group of older ladies standing near a cluster of potted palms and floral arrangements in a corner of the ballroom. The ladies watched them approach with somewhat puzzled expressions, until one of them, as they got closer, broke into a smile and stepped forward.

"My dear Lady Hardenwell! It has been so long since we've seen you! And this...?"

"Is my daughter, Lady Venetia. This is her first venture into society, as her come-out was delayed by our mourning for my husband... I do hope that you will all make her feel welcome."

Ventia curtsied, and tried to remember the names of the women, as her mother introduced each one that she knew, and the others introduced the few that her mother had not previously met. Most of them regarded her with pity, after a first shocked look, but one or two seemed almost offended by her appearance.

Those, she would need to watch.

"Of course. Some of us have our daughters here as well – they are dancing now – so many gentlemen seek their company."

The words were said innocently enough, but they struck to Venetia's heart – would anyone want to dance with her at all?

Her mother fell into conversation with the women, all discussing what had occurred in their lives since they had last seen each other, and Venetia simply stood there, watching. Some people glanced in her direction, but after a while the whispers died away, and they ignored her. Perhaps there would be introductions to others, to gentlemen, later?

After a short while, some young women were brought to where they were, on the arms of gentlemen, having obviously just finished dancing, and were introduced to Venetia and her mother. Their expressions, uniformly, showed that they found Venetia's scar horrifying – even though her hair was curled to fall slightly over it.

So, there would be no friendships there. It was what she had expected, even though she had hoped for better. The gentlemen had also merely glanced her way, then left the group, showing no interest in being introduced. So Venetia stepped back into the shade of the potted palms and pretended to be invisible. She watched everyone and everything, and attempted to discover the names and titles of the people she saw, based on hearing the women around her talk about them.

Even though her mother had shown her long lists of names in their copy of Debrett's, and explained, as much as she knew, who was related to who, Venetia found it all utterly overwhelming. There were so many names, so many faces to remember! Perhaps it was good that she could stand here, being mostly unnoticed, and attempt to memorise them all, before she actually had to speak to them.

After some time, she accepted the fact that she would likely not have the chance to even be introduced to any gentlemen that night, let alone dance. The younger men, as she watched them, seemed all very similar – immaculately attired, full of confidence and arrogance, and certain of their appeal to the young ladies. She did not find that type of arrogance appealing, at all. If they were all like that, the chances of her ever finding a man she might wish to marry were very small. Yet she had to do so, or come midwinter, they, and their tenants, would likely starve.

A shiver ran through her, and she studied them again, hoping to see something which might give her hope. Nothing did.

Then, as supper was called, and her mother turned to her, she saw, on the other side of the room, a man she had not noticed before. He was dressed as immaculately as all of the others, albeit more sedately, and with a black band on his sleeve which indicated that he was in half mourning, but he moved differently. She studied him, in the short while she had before the crowd of people blocked her view.

It was not that he lacked confidence – far from it – he moved with a fluid surety which she admired, but he seemed, somehow, apart from the others. He was not with a group of other men, indeed, he seemed completely alone. And what set him apart was that he appeared undisturbed by that fact. He looked, she thought, rather like he was doing as she was, and simply observing everyone around him.

He turned, and she saw his face directly for the first time. A small gasp escaped her, even as the crowds obscured him. His face was familiar, somehow. Yet she did not know how, or why.

She shook her head, and took her mother's arm as they made their way to the supper tables.

Once they had received small plates of food, they settled on some chairs with some of Lady Hardenwell's friends, who were talking amongst themselves about the men who might be possible matches for their daughters.

"...and then there's the Earl of Templewick. He's new to the title – still in half mourning – shocking, it was, his uncle, who was the previous Earl, and all of his family were taken off by the cholera, leaving this man the new Earl. His father was the second son, but he's a few years in the grave too, so it fell to this man. I've heard good things about him so far, although he's rather aloof, apparently. But so good looking! I will arrange an introduction somehow, for my dear girl really must meet him. There aren't many unmarried Earls who are young, good looking and not wastrels! Look, he's just over there – a fine figure of a man, I think!"

The others all expressed agreement, and Venetia turned her eyes to the man they spoke of, and discovered it to be the man she'd been watching before, the one who seemed so familiar. She wanted, in that instant, to meet him, to speak to him, to understand why he appeared to be so different. And she had the most peculiar feeling about him – she thought that he might not turn away from her scar with revulsion.

Why she should think that, she couldn't imagine, but think it she did.

Chapter Five

For all that she hadn't danced, hadn't done anything but simply stand and watch others, and occasionally engage in conversation, the Ball had been exhausting. Every look of disgust, or disdain, or pity, had drained her strength further. Now, as the door closed after Molly, who had helped her ready for sleep, and Venetia finally could lie in her bed, sleep was suddenly far away.

Instead, her mind replayed the evening, replayed every expression.

An hour later, when she was finally drifting on the edges of sleep, half dreaming, the persistent dream of the man who had sewn up her face seemed to merge with her recollections of the Ball. In that dreamlike state, she saw something which she had not recognised at the time – the man she had watched at the Ball, who had seemed so familiar, bore a more than passing resemblance to the man she had so regularly dreamed of, the man who, she believed, had saved her from an even worse scar.

That realisation jarred her back to wakefulness, and she sat up, thinking about it. Surely, there could be no link between them? What could an Earl, dressed in the height of elegant fashion, have in common with a groom who had been carrying out errands, dressed in clothing suited to the stables? She could not imagine how the resemblance might exist, unless it was purely coincidence.

It was, of course, always possible that the groom was an illegitimate son of the Earl's father – such things happened, fairly frequently, even though most were hushed up. She shook her head – perhaps she was simply imagining it. After all, nothing about the day of her fall was clear in her mind, so perhaps, despite her dreams ever since, her image of the man who had helped her was false, and he looked nothing like the Earl.

Sighing, she lay down again, and tried to think of other things. Sleep claimed her, for the day had truly exhausted her, but that sleep was still populated by dreams, dreams filled with a handsome face and deep brown eyes.

*****

Despite it being late autumn, there was a social event almost every night, and Morgan quickly realised that going about in society was an exercise in endurance, more than anything else. He persisted, keeping his expression and manner determinedly calm and polite, whilst avoiding the traps that the mothers of eligible young women set.

At every event, he watched those around him, and saw, over and over, examples of how shallow and unkind many of the people were. They might be the highest nobility, but in their treatment of others, they were frequently not at all noble. Perhaps his perspective had been distorted by years at war but, if so, he was glad of it – he did not wish to be as many of these people were.

What disturbed him most was the gossip, and the rather vicious mockery of those who did not meet the arbitrary standards of the doyennes of the *ton*. He did not find sharp tongued criticism amusing, and he found the way that the young women were treated most strange. They were discussed as men might discuss horses for sale at Tattersall's – a comparison of their features and capabilities, their breeding, their dowries and other attributes, but never any consideration of either their personalities or their personal interests.

It was as if they were not people at all, but simply assets to be sold or bargained with for the benefit of their fathers and families. He had known it was like this, for his mother had described it to him, but it had not seemed real until he stood amongst it.

Unless a girl was perfect of features, with a good figure, from a good family, and with a good dowry, her prospects were definitely minimal. That realisation made his own situation seem worse – people expected him to marry, for the Earldom needed an heir, and they expected him to approach marriage exactly the same way that these people around him did. He could not do so. The idea of marrying a woman when there was no affection between them was abhorrent to him, and he knew full well that a fair exterior was no guarantee of a beautiful character.

The more he saw, the more he pitied the girl whose face he had tried so hard to repair.

That thought ran through his mind as he bowed to yet another young Lady, at yet another Ball.

"Good Evening, Lady Portia. Might you have a dance free?"

She simpered, looking nervous, and nodded.

"I do, my Lord."

He took the proffered dance card and wrote his name beside the next available dance. There were quite a few, for this young woman was plain of countenance and, although reputed to have quite a good dowry, she was still not often sought out. He had made it a practice to discover such young women, and speak with them, dance with them, rather than pursuing the acknowledged beauties.

He handed the card back, and bowed again.

"Until then, my Lady."

He moved away, noting others who stood on the sidelines, the wallflowers, as they were called. Some looked hopeful, others seemed to withdraw into the shadows, despairing of ever being noticed. He had seen the same young women do so at a number of events now.

He walked across the room towards a small group of gentlemen – men whose acquaintance he had recently made, and whom he had, so far, found to be tolerable company. They were clustered together, talking, and there was some quiet laughter – exactly at what, he did not know. He reached them in time to hear a remark which led to more laughter, at least from some.

"...she's fine enough of figure, but the face... would you want to look at that every day? And the whisper is that her dowry is nowhere near enough to make putting up with it worthwhile. I'll be looking elsewhere, that's for certain, when I eventually get serious about marrying."

A second man nodded, and his words had Morgan following the direction of their gaze across the room.

"It's rather presumptuous of her to think that any man would marry her, with a scar like that – especially when there are so many other unblemished women to choose from."

The casual cruelty of those words took his breath away, making him sure that the man who had spoken, Lord Woodster, would not become a friend. The small group of young women whom the men were looking at stood close to some older ladies, who were deep in conversation. There were four girls, of varying heights and figures, but one was taller than the rest, and stood with a slight stiffness which suggested to Morgan that she really did not wish to be there at all.

It seemed that she was the one they spoke of, for Lord Canstead nodded in agreement with Lord Woodster.

"Indeed. Not only is there the scar, but she is very tall, and rather more lean than I like a woman to be."

Morgan studied her, hoping that the men would turn the conversation to other things, and planning to escape their company as soon as he could politely do so. As he watched, she turned her head, and the light fell directly on her face.

His heart skipped a beat.

Surely, it couldn't be her?

For the face he saw by that light was beautiful, surmounted by rich red brown hair and, on the forehead, only partially concealed by an artful fall of curls, was a scar – leaf shaped, and the dark reddish colour which suggested that it had been gained relatively recently. Could it be the same girl, the one he had spent so many hours on?

It seemed improbable, and yet... surely there could not be two women with a scar like that, in that exact location?

He stepped forward a little.

"I've not been introduced to any of them – who is she?"

Woodster turned to him.

"Perhaps it's best to avoid introductions – if you're not introduced, you can't be trapped into dancing with them. But if you really want the names, give me a moment to think... ah yes – the one with the scar is Lady Venetia... something. I believe she's the daughter of a Marquess, but lacks a dowry of appropriate size – at least that's what the gossip says."

He went on to give the names of two of the other young women, but Morgan barely heard them – his mind had stopped listening after gaining information about the girl with the scar. He admired her courage in being here, admired the fact that she managed to stand calmly in a room full of the *ton*, almost certainly knowing full well that she was being judged.

Curiosity filled him – what was she like, this young woman who had the courage to put her horse at near impossible jumps, to stand here in a room full of people guaranteed to disparage her? And... why was she here? She could have waited until the Spring before braving the ton, surely, thus giving her face more time to heal, and for the scar to fade. For her to be here now – and he realised that he had come to the conclusion that it was the same girl, that what he saw on that face was the result of his own handiwork – there must be some driving need.

He simply could not imagine a woman putting herself in such a position unless there was no other option.

Did he want to be introduced?

Or would that be unwise? Would she remember him – after all, she had been dazed, and then drugged with the laudanum, so it was likely that she had no recollection of the events of that day at all. And... what if it wasn't the same girl – what if it was his memory which was faulty?

Woodster did not seem to have noticed Morgan's distraction, for he went on speaking.

"Mind you, I doubt the dowry will come into it – with her face ruined like that, she's not likely to get any serious interest. The most she'll get is old men propositioning her to become their mistress – a woman disfigured is ruined for society marriage, and becomes fair game for the debauched hunters looking for nothing but their own pleasure. I wouldn't be interested, myself – I'm young enough that getting a mistress who isn't disfigured is easy – so why would I bother with the likes of her? But the old men – they only have their money to attract women with..."

A flood of anger rushed through Morgan, stealing his breath. He swallowed, striving for calm. Finally, Woodster was looking at him as if expecting some response. What could he say?

"I... I'll bear that in mind, Woodster. I've certainly no interest in being trapped – into dancing or anything more – by any of these women, scarred or not!"

Woodster clapped him on the back, cheerfully oblivious to the fury that Morgan repressed.

"That's the right attitude, Templewick. No point in being caught in the parson's mousetrap until you're good and ready."

He forced a false smile onto his face and, thankfully, the men turned their conversation to safer topics, like hunting and horses, which Morgan was well suited to discussing. Internally, his mind went over the previous conversation, even as his eyes repeatedly went back to the still figure of the girl across the room, and he berated himself for not having done a delicate enough job on her face. He had hoped to save her from this sort of disparagement, but he had, very obviously, failed.

*****

Each ball or soiree that they attended drove home to Venetia, even more, the fact that a scar on the face, however small, was enough to utterly change a girl's future, and her chances for happiness. There had been introductions to gentlemen, but very few had asked her to dance – and those who had done so tended to be older, and rather improper in their manner to her.

Her mother spoke only encouraging words, but Venetia could see the strain building in her, as the chance that Venetia would make a good match was revealed to be vanishingly small. There was, however, nothing to do but go on.

Beside her, her mother stiffened. Venetia turned slightly, looking for the cause, which was immediately obvious. A gentleman approached them. He was older, somewhat portly, and a little red in the face. His eyes were set upon them, and Venetia's stomach twisted. He did not appeal to her at all, but by his expression, he found her quite of interest.

Next to her mother, Lady Hallam paused in her conversation, and turned to see what had distracted Lady Hardenwell. The gentleman smiled at that and, coming to a stop in front of them, spoke first to Lady Hallam.

"My dear Lady Hallam, might I trouble you to introduce me to your friend and her... daughter?"

Lady Hallam seemed to find this a perfectly ordinary request, although Venetia rather wished that she had not been so accommodating.

"Why of course, my Lord." She turned to Lady Hardenwell and Venetia. "Lady Hardenwell, Lady Venetia, might I make known to you the Earl of Blatherfort? My Lord, this is the Dowager Lady Hardenwell, and her daughter, Lady Venetia Chater."

The Earl bowed, and Venetia curtsied in return.

As she did, her mind slipped to the man she had seen at that previous event, the Earl of Templewick – she would far rather be being introduced to that Earl, instead of this one!

"Delighted to meet you, ladies. Lady Venetia... might I hope for a dance?"

Venetia took a steadying breath. No matter how much she wanted to, she could not refuse him – not if she hoped to have any other gentleman dance with her.

"Of course, Lord Blatherfort. I have this next dance free."

And every other dance tonight...

At that moment, the orchestra struck up, and the man beamed at her, and offered her his arm. She placed her hand upon it, and allowed him to lead her to the floor, where others were forming up. The dance was to be one of the older style, with stately steps and a great deal of rotating about other dancers. She was glad of that, for she did not wish to have to be in contact with him any more than absolutely necessary.

He took her hand, and she could feel, even through her glove, that his was damp. It sent a little shiver of revulsion through her. They began to move, and as the steps called for him to draw her close, before turning her away, he spoke.

"You've a fine figure, my Lady but, if you'll forgive me for being blunt, your scar rather detracts from your... visual appeal. But I am not a man to be easily put off."

She gasped, but the dance spun her away around the next couple, and she was saved from making any immediate response as a result. But of course, the reprieve was only momentary – the dance brought them back together again all too soon.

"I'm sure that you're aware of how... limited... your prospects are, my Lady. In the matter of marriage, that is. But... if a gentleman seeks a Lady's companionship, without the complications of matrimony... well then, he is likely to be a little more... flexible... in his determinations. I am sure that you know what I mean."

Again, the dance saved her from the need for immediate response, and by the time it brought them back together, she was ready.

"I believe that I do understand exactly what you are implying, my Lord. And I must say now that I find your offer remarkably improper. I must decline it, I am afraid. Regardless of how you may perceive my situation, I still have the hope of something more... traditional... than the role of mistress."

The man had the gall to laugh at her words.

"Then the best of luck to you, my Lady – for you'll need it. When you're desperate, do come and call on me, and we'll see if I am in a generous mood – but of course, by then, some other woman may have taken advantage of my kindness..."

The dance, with a final set of turns about other couples, finally ended, and he led her back to her mother, who watched her approaching with worried eyes. Venetia suspected that her cheeks were flushed – from anger, not exertion.

Only once he had bowed and left them did Lady Hardenwell touch Venetia's hand.

"Venetia? Is all well? You look rather... flustered?"

"All is as well as is to be expected. I am sure that I will get used to being propositioned by arrogant men eventually. And perhaps I will improve the polish of my rejection speech to them, with more practice."

Lady Hardenwell slipped her arm through Venetia's.

"Oh, my dear girl! We will survive this, somehow. Amongst all of the gentlemen in London, surely there is at least one capable of seeing you as the treasure that you are, of looking past the surface? At least you are now being asked to dance, and that means you are seen, and others may dance with you too. So you must see the self-important bounders like Blatherfort as simply a tool to allow others to notice you."

"I truly hope that you are right, Mother, but it seems unlikely... and I will not accept an improper offer, regardless."

"Nor should you – even if we have to sell everything we have to survive, that is better than giving up all hope, and allowing a man like that to degrade you."

Venetia said nothing more, but the thoughts which ran through her mind were full of despair.

If we have to sell everything, then we will fall to a state of poverty where offers like Lord Blatherfort's may come to seem worthwhile...

Chapter Six

After the dreadful dance with Lord Blatherfort, Venetia stayed close to her mother and the group of other less popular young ladies and their mothers, glad that she had not been asked to dance the next dance, or the one after. The idea of dancing, if each dance might lead to being so tastelessly propositioned, had become far less appealing. Instead, she simply watched others, scanning the room, attempting to remember everyone's names, and studying the interactions between gentlemen and ladies.

Across the room, movement caught her eye. A group of mostly younger gentlemen stood talking, and they had just been joined by another. It seemed as if they were looking in her direction – but why would they? Then, as they moved a little, she caught a better view of the newcomer to their group and a little shiver of surprise ran through her.

It was him – Lord Templewick – the man she had noticed at a previous Ball. The man whose face seemed so like the face in her dreams...

She wanted, then, to find a way to go to him, to speak to him, to discover if there was any connection, any reason for him to seem so familiar, so like the man she half remembered, after her fall.

She shook her head, and turned her eyes away.

There could be no link between an Earl and a groom – she was simply indulging in wishful thinking, driven by her desire to meet the man who had done his best by her injury, and thank him for trying.

*****

It was late, and Venetia yawned inelegantly. Her mother shook her head.

"We should stop this conversation and go to bed. I think that we have a clear plan for the next week or so. There are so many events to attend... surely, at one of them, you will meet a man who is not instantly judgemental."

Venetia gave a grim smile.

"I am beginning to doubt that there are any gentlemen of that nature amongst the *ton*. But you are right – further discussion tonight will serve no purpose. I will just go to the library and select a book, to read myself to sleep. I will see you in our rooms shortly."

Her mother nodded, and gathered up the embroidery she had been working on as they talked.

The library was quiet, and Venetia went instantly to the section she wanted – it seemed that her uncle had changed nothing in the room, so she easily found her favourite books. She stood there for a moment, the scent of books wrapping around her, entangled with her memories of this house, this room, and a sense of hopelessness filled her. It was so unfair that she and her mother should have lost everything, and that her uncle cared not a whit for their wellbeing.

For a moment, tears made her vision blur, then she dashed them away with her fingers, reached out and selected a book, almost at random, and turned to leave the room. Everything in this house was a painful reminder, through her memories, every day, of her situation. Everything except Lord Jasper, who was simply painful.

Venetia avoided him constantly, and he, when he wasn't out carousing and gambling, seemed to take delight in bedevilling her. She had been careful not to let him catch her alone again, but he tried, and it was, she was sure, only a matter of time. What she would do then, she did not know.

She hurried up the stairs, the book clutched to her, the dark house around her suddenly feeling threatening. Halfway along the corridor to her rooms, it was as if a shadow detached itself from behind a statue which stood in a niche. She opened her mouth to scream as hands took her shoulders, wrenching her around, but the scream never escaped her, for lips came down upon hers, mercilessly taking a kiss from her.

She knew from the scent of him that it was Lord Jasper, and she struggled in his grasp. He, no doubt the wiser from their previous encounter, avoided her knee to his private parts, but he did not expect her to slam the edge of the book into that area. His mouth left hers, and she screamed then, hoping to be heard.

That hope was answered, when her mother's door opened, and Lady Hardenwell came rushing out into the corridor. Lord Jasper looked in her direction and cursed under his breath, at which point Venetia applied the book again, and found herself released as Lord Jasper crumpled in pain.

Her mother gave her a look of approval as she reached them, but immediately turned her full attention to Lord Jasper. Venetia recognised the look on her face – Lord Jasper was about to be chastised in a very thorough and pointed fashion.

"Lord Jasper! What is the meaning of this? How dare you accost my daughter in such an inappropriate way!"

Lord Jasper glared at her, struggling to speak. He dragged himself upright again, one hand still cupping his injured parts. His face twisted into a sneer.

"The slattern should be glad that any man wants to touch her, with a face marred like that! It was just a kiss – she should be pleased, rather than seeking to injure me!"

Lady Hardenwell regarded him with disgust - her voice, when she spoke again, was cold and hard, and she delivered her words with knife like precision.

"If you ever speak of my daughter like that again, I can guarantee that you will suffer far worse injury... both physically, and reputationally. Have you forgotten that I know about your debts? Would your father care to know of your debt to Lord Pidwenning?" Lord Jasper paled, and swallowed hard after a sharp intake of breath. "No? I didn't think so – you believed that I did not have the details? That was foolish of you. Perhaps your father would be interested in just how you acquired that debt – I do believe that it would tarnish his honour rather badly..."

"I... You can't..."

Lord Jasper spluttered to a stop in the face of Lady Hardenwell's implacable expression.

"I can. Very easily. And I will, unless your behaviour improves dramatically. Now get out of my sight, and think well on what I've said."

Lord Jasper backed away from her, as if she might strike him.

"You have no authority over me, Aunt. I could cast you from this house."

"You could... but only if you wish your reputation to be ruined in the eyes of society. If you act badly towards us, I will ensure that all of the worst gossips know all of your failings. I am sure that such juicy information would spread very quickly."

Lord Jasper looked as if he wanted to spit on them, but instead, he simply nodded.

"I see your point. You have the advantage for now. But I will not forget this. You will rue this day, I assure you."

He spun on his heel and went down towards the other end of the corridor, where the family rooms were located. His haughty exit was, however, rather ruined by the weaving path he took, as a result of too much drink, and the discomfort which she had inflicted on him with the book.

Venetia stood there beside her mother, and neither spoke until Lord Jasper was completely out of sight. Then Lady Hardenwell turned to her, placing a hand on her arm.

"Come into our sitting room, Venetia. We will ring for tea, even though it is late."

Venetia clutched the book to her, hoping that she had not damaged it when applying it as a weapon, and looked closely at her mother.

"Mother… how did you learn the specifics of his debt? And.. what did he do, that is so disreputable?"

Lady Hardenwell opened the door, and pushed Venetia towards the couch, then rang the bellpull before sitting beside her.

"I spoke to all of the most inveterate gossips I knew – never asking directly, but asking about the most scandalous things they'd heard in the last year – I claimed that I wanted to know more of what had been going on in society while we were in mourning. And I asked about scandal or whispers about gentlemen, claiming to be only concerned that you not become associated with an unsuitable man. And then I put all of the little pieces of information together, to discover a bigger picture."

"You are so clever – and I am so grateful that you are. Lord Jasper revolts me – surely… surely not all kisses are like that?"

Lady Hardenwell laughed.

"No, not all kisses are like that. Most kisses, if you actually want to be kissed by the man in question, are remarkably pleasant."

At that point, the tea tray arrived, and they let the conversation lapse.

It was only much later, as she drifted off to sleep, that Venetia realised that her mother hadn't told her exactly what scandalous things Lord Jasper had done, to incur that debt.

*****

The Ball was crowded, far more so than the last few he had attended, and Morgan allowed himself to be swept into various conversations between groups of gentlemen, some of whom he did not like at all, a few of whom he actually found to be decent, and the vast majority of whom seemed simply to be rather dull and self-absorbed, but not actively unpleasant.

Soon, however, he found himself in need of other amusement, for their conversation was centred around gambling – horse racing, to be precise – and Morgan had no wish to make the depth of his knowledge in the area of race horses known to the *ton*. He slipped away from them on the pretext of obtaining a drink, and instead went in search of a wallflower to dance with. By rarely speaking with the same girl twice, let alone dancing with her, he managed to not generate much gossip, and yet still bring some pleasure to their evenings.

Introductions could be difficult, but he had, in his first week in London, realised that his mother knew an inordinate number of people, far more than he had realised, and that she was perfectly happy to introduce him to those who could then introduce him to young ladies. He thought that she secretly hoped he would be taken with one of them, and marry, but she did not speak of it. She knew that he would come to it in his own time, and that pushing him would only delay it.

He surveyed the room, and noticed a cluster of young women to one side, most accompanied by their mothers. Amongst them, if he was not mistaken, was the girl with the scar.

Should he?

Curiosity drove him then, and he sought out his mother, drawing her a little away from the coterie of her friends.

"Mother, do you see the young Lady over near the large vase of roses? The taller one, with dark hair?"

"The one speaking to a shorter blonde girl?"

"Yes, that one. Do you know her? Or know someone who might introduce me?"

His mother regarded him with a smile.

"Is she to be your 'charitable endeavour' for the evening?"

Morgan felt his cheeks flush.

"I do not know that I would put it quite that way, Mother... but yes, in effect, that is true, if she chooses to converse, or dance, with me."

Lady Anna Follett knew almost everyone, for despite having married a younger son, with no title of his own at the time, she was of course, still entitled to the designation of 'Lady Anna' that she had been born to. As the daughter of a Duke, she was welcome everywhere in society – especially now that her son had succeeded to the title of Earl of Templewick – and she took full advantage of the fact.

She laughed at his rather stiff reply, and waved a hand dismissively.

"Of course she will – any of them would, if you gave them attention! But come, let us find Lady Cotteridge – I believe that she knows the girl's mother."

With that, she set off, leaving Morgan to follow. Lady Cotteridge, it seemed, most definitely did know the Lady in question.

But, having confirmed that, Lady Cotteridge frowned and, after a moment's hesitation, spoke again.

"I can certainly introduce you, if you wish it, but... I must warn you – the young Lady has an unfortunate scar upon her face, and many regard her as ruined by that, as unsuitable to marry any gentleman of breeding. I pity her – her father was a good man, but his death sent the title to her uncle, and I believe that she and her mother live on a relatively small annuity. It is whispered that her dowry is minimal – far less than one might expect for a Marquess' daughter. When that combines with the scar, I doubt that she has much in the way of prospects..."

Morgan clenched his jaw, saddened and angered by the way in which society dismissed her, even though Lady Cotteridge had spoken with some kindness in her tone. His mother looked to him with a questioning expression.

"I would still seek an introduction, my Lady – I do not judge people by physical appearance alone."

Lady Cotteridge gave what seemed a pleased nod.

"Then follow me, and I shall grant you that introduction."

They walked around the edges of the room until they reached the group of women. As they approached, some noticed, and the conversation in the group stopped – all eyes were turned to Morgan and curiosity was obvious on each face. Curiosity and hope.

Lady Cotteridge stopped in front of an older, but still beautiful woman, who stood near the scarred girl.

"Lady Hardenwell, might I make known to you the Earl of Templewick? He is but recently, and unexpectedly, come into his title, and I am making an effort to introduce him to as many people as possible. No doubt he will struggle to remember all of the names, but we must give him the chance!"

She gave a soft laugh, as did Lady Hardenwell, who then turned to Morgan.

"I am happy to be made known to you, my Lord. Our year of mourning has left me quite out of touch!"

Morgan bowed.

"I am delighted to make your acquaintance, my Lady."

She nodded, then drew the girl forward.

"And this is my daughter, Lady Venetia."

The girl curtsied, and Morgan bowed again, taking her hand for a moment. The warmth of it shocked him, and he brought startled eyes to her face. Her eyes were the rich green of summer leaves, and he felt as if he was falling into them. The scar, whilst he noted it peripherally, seemed unimportant, compared to those beautiful eyes.

For moments, they simply stared at each other, before she flushed and looked down, and he released her hand.

"Delighted, Lady Venetia. Would you... would you perhaps care to dance?"

She looked quite shocked, and around them, all of the other young women whispered, apparently startled by his asking. Her voice shook very slightly when she answered.

"Most certainly, my Lord, I am very fond of dancing."

Feeling the pressure of all of the other eyes upon him, Morgan turned to Lady Cotteridge again.

"And of course, I must press Lady Cotteridge to introduce me to all of the other beautiful young ladies who surround me."

It was as if they all collectively relaxed. Lady Cotteridge smiled at him, approvingly, no doubt thinking that he spoke only out of kindness. Which was true, in a way – but it was also true that he hoped to discover women who had good conversation, as well as visual appeal.

"Of course, my Lord, of course."

Introductions proceeded, and when the dance which Lady Venetia had granted him was called, he was greatly relieved to be able to step away from all of the attention. In the end, he knew that, of them all, she was the only one he truly cared to get to know better. There was just something about her....

*****

"They're coming this way!"

Venetia turned at the excited whisper from Miss Julia MIllwood, as did all of the others in the little group of wallflowers.

"Who?"

But even as she asked she saw... it was him! The Earl of Templewick was following Lady Cotteridge towards them – it was quite clear that the group she stood in was his destination.

Her heart pounded, and her mouth was suddenly dry. Lady Cotteridge led the Earl, and an older woman, directly to where Venetia stood with her mother – there was no mistaking it – they were the target of her attention.

Lady Cotteridge made introductions, and Venetia curtsied when required, wondering why this introduction was being made. Then, all thought was stolen from her, for the Earl took her hand and bowed.

The heat of that contact flowed through her, and as he rose from the bow, her eyes met his. It was as if she was in one of her dreams – she was drowning in those deep brown pools, drowning in an expression which contained only kindness, and nothing of disgust or disdain. Yet he had seen her scar, he must have, this close to her!

She felt oddly connected to him, as if she had always known him, as if she could speak of anything to him, and be heard.

But that was ridiculous – and she realised that she had been staring at him for too long. She turned her eyes away as she felt the flush rise in her cheeks. Breaking eye contact seemed to release him from the spell of stillness which had held them, and his fingers dropped from her hand. She missed the contact acutely, and the room felt suddenly colder for its lack.

Then, he startled her again – rather than moving on to speaking to others, he stayed with her, and moments later asked her to dance. As he did, she heard a sharp intake of breath from every other young Lady near them. Quickly, she accepted – she would be an utter fool to not take this chance!

But he must have noticed the other girls reactions, for he asked Lady Cotteridge to introduce them all. It was an act of great kindness, yet she almost wished that he hadn't, for she found that she wanted to feel as if he wanted to be with her alone.

Chapter Seven

He led her to the dance floor without hesitation, and they took up their positions as the music began. This dance started with them facing each other, one hand linked. He looked at her, truly looked at her, rather than avoiding her face, and a shocking thrill went through her. All her life, people had looked at her like this, and she had never appreciated it, until now, after weeks of people flinching from the sight of her scar.

For a moment she was on the edge of tears from gratitude. Then she drew in a breath as they began to move, and collected herself. What puzzled her most was why he did not react as others did – why could he look at her scar without being horrified by it?

Could it be because... because he knew it would be there? Because he had seen it before....?

But surely he could not be the man who had sewn it...

She was drawing mad conclusions from the fact that he was kind, after so many had been cruel. Mentally, she gave herself a shake – she should be sensible, and simply enjoy the moment and not allow herself to create wishful dreams. It was a moment worth enjoying, for he danced well.

The dance brought them face to face again, and he smiled.

"Do you enjoy social occasions, Lady Venetia?"

Should she tell him the truth? She wanted to...

"I... have not been about in society much, my Lord – my come-out was delayed by our mourning for my father – so I do not really know if I might enjoy such things. So far, my experience has been... not as pleasant as I had hoped."

They turned, and a little frown crossed his face.

"I do hope that I am improving that situation, rather than making it worse?"

He sounded as if he actually cared! Venetia laughed softly, utterly captivated by the attention of a man who seemed to consider her feelings.

"You are indeed improving the situation, my Lord."

He smiled then.

"I am relieved to hear it. I fear that, after all of those introductions, I will be rather busy dancing with many young ladies – but perhaps we might dance again at the next Ball we both attend, without causing gossip?"

Venetia found that her mouth was suddenly dry – so dry that she could not speak. He wanted to dance with her again? Was that really what he had just suggested? A bubble of happiness rose within her – perhaps, just perhaps, she was not so utterly doomed as she had thought.

"Yes, I would enjoy dancing with you again. But... I... I did not expect that you would be so kind as to dance with all of those to whom you were introduced. Most gentlemen are not so courteous..."

As soon as she spoke, she wished that she hadn't, for it was a very forward and improper thing to have said! But, rather than looking annoyed as she had expected, he gave a wry smile.

"I fear that I do not fit the common behaviour of most gentlemen of the *ton*. I have spent much of my life away from society."

That was curious. Where had he spent his life? She remembered, then, the conversation of the older ladies, where one had remarked that he had come into his title unexpectedly, when his uncle and the uncle's whole family had died. What had he done, where had he been, before he became Earl? She wanted to know, but it was most rude and improper to even consider asking. So she asked nothing about it.

"I, for one, prefer your conversation and manner to that of most gentlemen of the *ton*, so perhaps, being different is not a bad thing?"

He gave a soft laugh then.

"I am glad that you think so."

At that point, the dance came to an end, and her opportunity for conversation was removed. They walked back to her mother, and she wondered if he had truly meant the suggestion that they should dance again. She hoped that he had, rather desperately.

They stopped, and the cluster of other young ladies watched as he released her and bowed, their expressions hopeful, and almost predatory. In that moment, she almost pitied him, for if he intended to dance with each one of them, then he would be subject to a variety of conversation, and no doubt to some degree of future hopefulness as well. Would his kindness be strong enough to carry him through all of it?

And, most importantly of all, would he want to dance with any of them again, or was that honour reserved only for Venetia?

*****

The dance had gone well, he thought, although he wished that he had been able to be a better conversationalist. Yet another skill which he had not really needed, in his previous life! Yet she had seemed happy – indeed there had been a moment at the beginning of the dance when a smile had lit her face, making her truly beautiful, in a manner that no scar could diminish.

He just wished that he understood what he had done to cause that smile.

She was, far more than any of the other young women, fascinating. He had enjoyed dancing with her, in a way that he had not with any other young Lady so far. Which was what had motivated him to suggest that they dance again at another event. To do so went against his usual approach to things, for it risked his name being linked with hers, yet he could not regret it – indeed, he rather looked forward to that future dance.

He had, as they danced, considered that scar – more and more, as he looked at it, he was sure that it was his handiwork, that this was the young Lady who he had worked on that day in June. He would like to have that fact confirmed – yet how could he do so? He could not ask her outright about it – that would be the height of rudeness, especially as he might be wrong, this might be a different young woman. His mind worried at the puzzle of it, but he could see no way to politely discover the truth.

He was intrigued by her comment that she found his company more appealing than most men of the *ton* – for he did not think himself to compare well to most of them, not after years at war, and years as a country stablemaster! Yet she had seemed most genuine in the remark. It was a kindness on her part, and it caused a warmth to grow within him.

The dance came to a close, and he led her back to her mother – and the waiting collection of wallflowers. His own mother was in conversation with Lady Hardenwell, but she raised an eyebrow in his direction, which he pretended not to notice at all.

Lady Venetia removed her hand from his arm and curtsied.

"Thank you, my Lord."

He bowed.

"It was delightful."

He meant the words, he realised. She flushed slightly, and dropped her eyes, turning towards her mother.

Morgan stepped away, and found himself confronted by the hopeful gazes of the other young women. He forced a bland smile to his face, and chose the most nervous looking one to approach for the next dance. He had not expected going about in society to provide him with much exercise, but he was beginning to realise that he was wrong in that assumption – he was going to dance enough to keep himself fit, at this rate.

*****

Morgan settled back into the well-padded seats of the carriage with a sigh. It had been a long evening, and he was shocked to discover just how much his feet hurt, and his muscles complained of all the dancing that he had done. Opposite him, his mother smiled.

"Tired, Morgan?"

"Very. If you'd told me three months ago that dancing could be this much of a physical effort, I wouldn't have believed you."

His mother laughed, shaking her head.

"It's a very different kind of exercise from training horses, isn't it? But you'll adapt. Have any of these young women you've been dancing with attracted your interest, yet? Or are they all still just charity cases to you? And, by the way, I approve of that, as an approach – all of them deserve to be treated kindly and to garner some attention, even if they are not the most beautiful. But... am I mistaken – I rather thought that tonight you seemed more interested in Lady Hardenwell's daughter than in any of the others."

Instinct nearly sent him to speaking an immediate denial, but his innate honesty stopped the words before they left his lips. For he had to admit, if only to himself, that he had found Lady Venetia far more interesting than any of the other young women he had so far met, if only because she had spoken so plainly, without artifice. He had not, at any point, felt that she was assessing him as a potential husband.

And that was a relief – not that he objected to the idea of being seen as worth marrying, but he did dislike the rather obvious and predatory way that many young ladies seemed to approach it. Although… it was much the same way that the gentlemen assessed the young ladies, he supposed.

His mother was waiting for an answer, and he realised that he had delayed too long.

"I would not say that I am interested, in the way that you no doubt hope for, but she was most definitely more entertaining to speak to, and to dance with, than most. She did not simper, and she spoke plainly, without sickly attempts to charm me. Which meant that the dance was pleasant, rather than an exercise in strained politeness."

His mother had a little half smile on her face, and he suspected that she was entertaining hopes… but when she spoke again, she surprised him, for it was not about his potential for marrying, as he'd thought it might be, but more focussed on Lady Venetia herself.

"And… you didn't find the scar on her face off-putting? Most people seem to, which is unfortunate for the poor girl."

Morgan met his mother's eyes – eyes a deep dark golden brown like his own – as he considered his answer.

"No, I didn't see it as disfiguring. She has a beautiful face, and rich green eyes – the scar doesn't change any of that. I long ago learnt that the beauty of what is on the outside does not always reflect what is on the inside, and equally, a marred exterior does not mean that what is inside is not beautiful. Character is far more important than appearance."

She nodded, obviously pleased by his words.

"You are wise – far wiser than most young men of the *ton*. I am glad of it – you have grown into a man I can be proud of."

Morgan felt a flush rise in his face at the unexpected praise. Perhaps he wasn't doing such a bad job of dealing with society after all…

"Thank you."

After that, they lapsed into silence, as the carriage conveyed them home.

He thought, as the cobbles rumbled by under the wheels, about what he had said, and about how he had felt, dancing with her. It truly had been pleasant – and he had meant it when he had suggested that he would dance with her again, soon. He wanted to, which startled him a little.

He was even looking forward to it.

*****

That night, for the first time, the man in her dreams was more defined, more the Earl she had danced with, than the vague impression of the groom she had held in her mind for months. The two merged in the dream, both kind and considerate, as if they were the same, despite all of the differences.

Because in one thing, she was absolutely certain, they were the same – they both looked at her face directly, with no hint of disgust or aversion.

That fact fed the small flame of hope within her, the flame which had been close to flickering out, and gave it strength to go on. If one man could look at her without revulsion, then surely so could others. Perhaps she might still find a man to marry, after all?

Venetia slipped into deeper sleep on that thought, wishing that the day when she might dance with the Earl of Templewick again was already here.

*****

Three long weeks had passed, and October was nearly gone – the days had closed in, and the taste of winter was in the air. The talk amongst society was of who would retreat to their country estates for Christmastide, and when they might go. If anything, the social events became more frenetic, as if everyone wanted to enjoy themselves before the colder weather made that more difficult.

Her uncle and aunt had returned from Hard Abbey, stayed two weeks, and departed again, declaring London too dull, when all of those who were their preferred company had retreated to the countryside already. Venetia could not say that she was sorry to see them go. Her uncle was an unpleasant man, as self-interested in his own way as his son, and her aunt agreed with whatever her husband said and did, having seemingly no personality of her own.

At least it left them with the house mostly to themselves, except when Lord Jasper chose to show his face – which wasn't often, thankfully, not since that last incident when Lady Hardenwell had threatened him with detailed exposure to the gossips, and his father.

On this particular afternoon, Venetia and her mother sat in their small sitting room in Hardenwell House, where a fire kept the chill at bay.

Lady Hardenwell looked pensive, and Venetia wondered just what she was thinking about. She sipped her cup of warm chocolate and stared at the flames, waiting for her mother to speak.

Long minutes passed, and the silence remained, such that Venetia felt almost close to drifting off to sleep in her chair. She was startled back to full attention when Lady Hardenwell spoke.

"By the end of November, nearly everyone will have left London, retreating to their country homes before the roads get so bad as to make travel difficult. If... if you have not made a match by that time, then we must retreat too, and go back to Brightwood Chase. I do not think that we will have a pleasant Christmas, for we will have to economise excessively. There isn't a gentleman that you might...?"

Venetia set her cup down, shaking her head gently.

"There isn't – and it's not a matter of 'a gentleman I would consider' so much as 'a gentleman who would consider me'. One who isn't lecherous, excessively old, a gambler and wastrel, or all of those together, that is. We must face it, Mother – this scar has, indeed, been the ruin of me. No man will consider me as a wife. I… I am so sorry…" her voice broke a little, and a sob escaped her, but she forced herself to go on. "It is all my fault. You were right, every single time that you told me I was rash and foolish. I never thought that it could come to this… But I brought this on myself, and I will bear it. I am only sorry that it places such a burden on you as well."

Lady Hardenwell reached across and took her hand, squeezing her fingers gently.

"We will survive, somehow. Perhaps tonight you will meet someone, or…."

"I doubt it, Mother, but still, I will try."

"Then we had best get dressed and ready ourselves for tonight's Ball, if you are to have the best possible chance…"

Venetia rose, sighing.

"You're right. I'll ring for Molly and get started."

Three hours later, they were on their way downstairs, with the carriage waiting outside, when Lord Jasper stepped into the front hall. He looked them over superciliously, and a shiver of dread went through Venetia. She did not know why, for surely there was nothing he could do in the current situation, except sneer at her, yet she shivered a little, regardless.

They stopped. It was only polite that they greet him.

"Good evening, Lord Jasper. I see that you are on your way out – to the same Ball that we are attending? Or to another event?"

For a moment, Venetia was taken aback by her mother's words – Lord Jasper had not yet attended even one of the events which they had been to. She suspected that he frequented gambling hells, or his club, but rarely anything more respectable. His expression became even more disparaging, and he laughed.

"I am going out, yes, but not to such uninspiring entertainment as Lady Quilpie's Ball. And as to you attending... I don't know why you bother - not even those dull dogs who attend Balls like that will sniff in your direction – haven't you accepted, yet, the fact that you're ruined for any decent man? You'd best choose whose mistress you'll be, while some are still interested, or you'll never be looked at, at all. But don't let me delay you, if you wish to continue with your farcical hopes."

And with those words, he bowed, and swept out through the door, to where his carriage waited near theirs. Venetia swallowed hard, for a moment close to tears, then she stiffened her resolve.

She would not allow Lord Jasper's unpleasantness to hurt her – she must try, must believe that she had some hope of finding a gentleman to marry.

But as they climbed up into the carriage, her fingers went to her face, momentarily tracing the outline of the scar, and doubt assailed her.

Chapter Eight

Somehow, despite his best intentions, three weeks had passed since the evening when he had danced with Lady Venetia. He had seen her at various events in that time, had looked directly at her and smiled, yet he had not found the time to be right to ask her to dance again. Truth be told, he rather thought that he was avoiding it – not because he didn't wish to dance with her, but more the opposite. He wanted to do so, and that shocked him a little.

But he could not do so too soon, or people would talk – and his mother would become even more convinced that there was more to it than there was. Instead, he danced with a never-ending stream of wallflowers, bringing momentary joy to the dreary lives of those not deemed to meet the highest standards of beauty. But he was becoming less and less enthusiastic about doing such acts of kindness.

They all looked at him hopefully, and he knew that he would disappoint them all, that, in a sense, he was falsely leading them on. And still, the only one he'd felt the least bit of interest in talking to, in dancing with again, was Lady Venetia. Perhaps it was time for him to actually do so, even if people would talk. It would give him the chance to see if she was still as interesting and... it would, perhaps, give him the chance to find out if she really was the girl whose face he had sewn up that June day.

As Mullard finished tying his cravat, Morgan resolved to seek Lady Venetia out that very night, to dance with her again, and to attempt to find a way to enquire about the scar, without being utterly, unmitigatedly, rude.

*****

It was, as Venetia had expected, just like all of the previous Balls. People flinched from looking directly at her, then whispered about her, usually obviously, and few would talk to her, apart from her mother's friends and some of their daughters. Given the chance, she spoke as cheerfully as possible, but when the conversation was a commiseration between other young ladies who were also overlooked by the gentlemen, it was in no way encouraging.

She danced twice, and each time it was with an older man, who promptly offered her the 'opportunity' to be his mistress. She was really getting rather tired of their persistence, and seeing their shocked looks when she refused.

After a short while, she simply stopped speaking with anyone, and watched the other people in the room – she had learnt rather a lot about many people, just by observing them at multiple social events. There were gentlemen whom she had never spoken to, yet who she knew she did not ever wish to be introduced to. There were ladies whose greatest delight was gossip, of the kind designed to be cruel to others, so that the gossiper might look better by comparison. And there were those she did not entirely understand – like the Earl of Templewick.

That dance with him stayed in her thoughts, but she was beginning to think that the second dance he had suggested might never happen. Surely three weeks was long enough... But perhaps he simply sought to protect both of them from gossip? She shook her head – it was best that she not indulge in fanciful thinking – he almost certainly simply wasn't interested in speaking or dancing with her again, and his words on that other night had been kindness with no substance behind it.

Even as she considered that idea, her reverie was shattered by a voice from beside her.

"Lady Venetia?"

She spun on the spot, her heart pounding.

It was him! The Earl of Templewick.

"I.. yes...?"

She sounded quite lack-witted! A flush came to her cheeks – what must he think of her? But he smiled, meeting her eyes, looking directly at her face again.

"I do apologise for startling you – you must have been deep in thought?"

"I was... I was considering..."

But no! she couldn't say that! Couldn't tell him that she had been watching what everyone else was doing – for to do so, so obviously, was most impolite. Her words failed her – what could she say now? He smiled again, and the sight of it made her heart pound for an entirely different reason, as heat rose within her.

"All of the people here? What they are doing, and saying, and why? Trying to make sense of it all?"

Venetia's head spun. He understood – he actually understood, and appeared not to find her actions improper!

"I... ah... yes, that is indeed what I was doing. Even though it is remarkably unladylike to admit to such a thing, I cannot deny it."

"I appreciate your honesty – for I must say that I often find the things that people do at social events to be somewhat nonsensical, and nearly always narrow-minded and self-centred. But I shouldn't admit to that, should I? One is supposed to pretend to not care, whilst avidly discovering whatever one can about other people's secrets, isn't one?"

Her mouth was dry, and an odd shiver ran through her. This was like no conversation she'd ever had before, and she thought that she liked it, for it was all of being forthright, and nothing of nastiness or subterfuge.

"Indeed, that is a good summation of how things seem to work. Although my experience of it is limited, and rather biased by the fact that the scar on my face causes a whole extra layer of... judgement... in how people interact with me."

He frowned, and she wondered if she had gone too far with her honesty, but then he nodded.

"I can see that it does. And it should not – such things should not be used to assess a person's character. But let me ask you what I came to you to ask – will you grant me a dance, Lady Venetia?"

A bubble of irrepressible hope rose within her. He had not forgotten! He had really meant it!

"I would be delighted to do so, Lord Templewick."

As if conspiring to improve her evening, the orchestra at that moment struck up for the next dance. Lord Templewick offered her his arm, and, with a glance in her mother's direction, she allowed him to lead her away.

Lady Hardenwell was smiling, and Venetia suspected that her mother's hopefulness was even greater than her own.

They joined the other dancers forming up, and only then did she realise that it was to be a waltz - which filled her with both delight and consternation. To be held so close in a gentleman's arms was a thrilling idea, yet it meant that he would be so very close that he could not help but see every detail of her scar, despite strategically placed curls, and the delicate application of face powder.

But... perhaps all would be well, for had they not just actually mentioned her scar, without him appearing in any way disconcerted?

The dance began, and Venetia found herself swept along with him, the steps coming easily. She looked up and met his eyes, their rich brown depths drawing her in, so that, for a moment, everything else seemed to fade away. They moved, carried by the music, without speaking at all, for what seemed like hours, although she knew it to be merely minutes. Eventually, however, he turned his eyes away from hers, almost as if a little uncomfortable. She felt the loss of that contact, intensely.

"Lady Venetia... you spoke, just now, of your scar, and the impact which it has had on how people treat you. Might I ask you a question?"

A shiver ran through her – was it wise to allow this conversation to proceed? Yet she could not really object, for she was the one who had first mentioned her scar.

"Yes, you may."

They swirled around the floor, and he said nothing immediately, as if choosing his words with care. Every second of silence drove her nervousness higher, and she castigated herself for a fool to have allowed this conversation to happen. But she could not stop it now.

"Lady Venetia, how did you come by that scar? For it appears to me perhaps to be rather recent. If I pry too far, please tell me – you need not feed my curiosity unless you truly wish to."

It was, absolutely, not the sort of question that a gentleman should ask a Lady! Yet she found herself not offended, somehow, because it was this man who asked. There was nothing prurient in his interest, nothing which spoke of a hope for a salacious gossip feeding tale – she had the impression that he was genuinely, simply, interested to know.

But that didn't mean she was going to tell him the whole sordid and embarrassing story. It was bad enough that she knew just how extraordinarily foolish she had been – she did not need to lay that out for the only gentlemen who had shown her any kindness, the only man she actually liked – for like him she did.

"I... do not really wish to speak about it, my Lord. Suffice it to say that I made a rash decision, and have paid the price for it." He nodded, and met her eyes again, searching with his gaze, as if he might see there the answer she had not given him. It made her want to know more about him, in turn, this man who did not outright reject her, who was so different from all of the others. "My Lord, I would ask a question of you in turn."

A smile crossed his lips then, and her eyes went to them, taking in their perfect shape. She licked her own lips in turn, mouth suddenly dry again. He was a most handsome man.

"Certainly, do ask, my Lady. I reserve the right to be as conservative in my answer as you were in yours."

Conservative! That was amusing- she would have described it as actively avoidant!

"I have heard it said, my Lord, that you have only recently come into your title, unexpectedly. The gossip suggests that you are an excellent manager of your estates – many good things are said – but nothing is spoken of about your life before the title descended upon you. You yourself have said that you have spent much of your life away from society. Which brings me to my question – if not amongst society, where have you spent your life? For to me, you seem quite different from most gentlemen."

*****

Morgan concentrated on the figures of the dance for a few moments, as the shock of her question ran through him. How could he answer that, without revealing things which he did not want society gossiping about? It was inevitable that they would learn more of his life eventually, but he wanted to delay that for as long as possible – there was quite enough attention focussed on him already, simply because he was an unmarried Earl, without adding to it!

And... if he told her the truth, what would she think of him?

For he had discovered that he cared what she thought of him, quite acutely.

If she was, as he believed, the young Lady whose face he had sewn up, then would she turn away from him, once she knew that he was one and the same as the groom who had helped her that day? Would that less than aristocratic part of his life horrify her? Weren't young ladies brought up to expect only gentlemen of the highest stratum of society to be suitable people to associate with, to potentially marry?

Marry...

The word dropped into his thoughts like a stone into a pond, causing ripples of other thoughts to spread from it.

Why should he think of that word, when considering the opinions of this young Lady in particular?

He pushed that question aside for later consideration, and concentrated on finding something to say, now.

"I... I was not in the direct line of inheritance for the title, which meant that my life followed, at least at first, the sort of path you might expect for a man nobly born but not of great significance. The sort of path which is generally a choice between the church, the military, law, or academia. But then fate caused me to cross paths with very different opportunities, so I took them. I was quite happy in that life, and I learnt many useful things – but very few of the things which society places value upon. Coming into the title has forced me to learn an entirely new way of life – which I am still adapting to."

There – hopefully she would accept that, for it was true, without actually revealing anything.

The music slowed a little, the flourishes leading them to the last turns of the dance, and he trained his eyes on her beautiful face again, assessing her response to his words. Her lips twisted into a wry smile, and for a moment he felt the impulse to bend the small distance between them and kiss those lips. The desire ran through him like lightning, shocking, unexpected.

"You have, indeed, risen to the challenge of being as conservative with your answer as I was with mine. You must realise, of course, that this just makes me all the more intrigued. I will have to forgive you for tonight, sadly, as the dance is ending – perhaps a future conversation will allow us to both edge closer to clarity...?"

Her words sent a thrill through him, for they suggested an ongoing dalliance, even if only of words, an ongoing opportunity to discover more about her, and perhaps, one day, to see if she remembered his fingers on her face.

“I would be delighted to indulge in a future conversation...” the music stopped, and he twirled her to a stop. They bowed and curtsied, and he offered his arm, “and another dance, perhaps?”

She blushed, and he wondered what she was thinking. He led her back towards her mother, and the cluster of hopeful young ladies. Waiting there, his eyes on Lady Venetia, was Lord Blatherfort. Beside him, she gave the smallest shudder, and Morgan thought that he understood.

“Yes, most definitely. I do enjoy dancing with you...”

He bent slightly closer to her, so that his words would reach only her.

“...whilst you do not enjoy dancing with gentlemen like Lord Blatherfort, who awaits you now?”

She faltered in her steps, just fractionally, then went on smoothly, a false smile on her face as she whispered an answer.

“Indeed, you have the right of it there. There is nothing to enjoy about being improperly propositioned by a man who is far too free with his hands on the dancefloor.”

Anger filled him, on her behalf.

“I must hope that such behaviour is not common.”

She gave the slightest bitter laugh.

“He will only be the third one this evening. So it rather depends on what you consider common, doesn’t it?”

*****

Venetia sat quietly on a chair near the end of a row, watching as the pianist settled. The evening was a musical soiree at Lady Thornmont’s home, and Venetia was cautiously optimistic – whilst the three young ladies who were to sing might not necessarily be talented, at least there were none of the old lechers in attendance.

The Countess of Thornmont called for attention, and the room quieted. A few latecomers slipped in as she began to speak, one sitting right beside Venetia. She did not look to see who it was, but politely concentrated on Lady Thornmont.

"Welcome to our musicale! Tonight, there are three parts to the evening – three different talented singers to entertain you, ably supported by Mr Chatterham on the pianoforte. First we have my daughter, Lady Anne Parry."

There was a polite smattering of applause as Lady Anne stepped up onto the stage, and Venetia steeled herself for the first notes – for if Lady Anne did not sing well, then the next half hour was most likely to be more like torture than pleasure. The pianist began, and moments later, Lady Anne's voice joined the music.

Venetia sighed in relief, for Lady Anne had a lovely voice, and the piece was chosen well to suit her. From beside her, the person who had slipped into the seat at the last minute spoke in a deep resonant whisper.

"A sigh of relief, no doubt, for one never knows what quality of song may issue forth..."

Venetia snapped her head around, to discover the Earl of Templewick, who had a wicked grin on his face. His eyes sparkled with what was surely mischief!

"Whether that is the case or not, it is most improper of you to suggest that it might be..."

Her whisper was very low, but he obviously heard, and his smile widened.

"Ah, but we have already established that I do not always behave in the manner which you might expect from a gentleman of the *ton* – although I do hope that you do not find me... unpleasantly improper...?"

She wanted to laugh, as a feeling of giddy delight in his company filled her. So she determinedly repressed that impulse, turned her eyes back to the young Lady performing, and issued what she hoped was a quelling "shhhh!"

Obediently, he ceased talking, but she was acutely aware of his presence, so very close beside her. Lady Thornmont's drawing room was not all that large, and the chairs were placed rather close together, which meant that she could almost feel the warmth of him – which made it remarkably difficult to concentrate on the performance. A performance which seemed to go on forever, no matter how talented Lady Anne was.

Venetia was greatly relieved when she concluded, and Lady Thornmont stated that there would be a fifteen-minute break before the next singer. But of course, that meant that she now had no excuse to avoid conversing with Lord Templewick...

"Do you enjoy musicales, Lady Venetia? Are they, perhaps, more to your taste than Balls?"

Venetia glanced sideways, towards her mother, and discovered that she was speaking to one of her friends, which allowed Venetia the chance to turn her full attention to Lord Templewick, and speak, knowing that there was very little chance that her mother would overhear.

"That rather depends, my Lord."

"Upon what does it depend?"

"Whether the talents of the performers are so poor as to cancel out the value of the fact that it seems that lechers seeking mistresses do not like music."

He laughed – a laugh which would have been large and delighted, had he been outside – a laugh which he barely managed to swallow into a sound constrained enough for a smallish drawing room.

"An interesting scale of assessment. I must ask you, at the end of the evening, to tell me where tonight falls, in your opinion."

She smiled at him, an odd bubble of happiness filling her.

"I will be delighted to provide you with a report."

Chapter Nine

Morgan had been half of a mind to not attend the musicale, for such things were often excruciatingly dull, or acutely painful to the ear, but he had, at the last minute, changed his mind. At a musicale, there was the chance to observe others in different situations, and to speak to various young ladies without the requirement to dance – his feet would appreciate the rest!

He had arrived just as the performance was about to start, and slipped into the room, taking the last vacant chair – which was, he discovered, beside Lady Venetia. It was as if he was meant to cross her path. It also, yet again, brought home to him just how much the scar affected how people treated her, for to be made the last person that anyone chose to sit beside was a dreadful cruelty.

When she had sighed in relief as the first performer proved to be tolerable, he had been unable to resist speaking to her, albeit as quietly as he could. She responded with her usual wit – words designed to sound perfectly proper, yet spoken in a tone which carried mischief in it. But she also determinedly quashed all conversation until after the singer had finished.

Now, as others rose and walked about in the break between performers, he chose to stay, and engage her in further conversation.

When he began with a rather inane question, she somehow turned it into something interesting, her sharpness drawing a laugh from him, unexpectedly – a laugh better suited to the stable yard, in its volume, which he'd had to quickly repress, lest he offend the people around him.

But the next part of the conversation pleased him greatly, for it provided an opportunity to suggest that they speak again, and soon. The idea of that delighted him, rather more than he had expected. He realised, with some small surprise, that he had come to enjoy her company, to look forward to speaking with her. It had crept up on him, yet now that he recognised it, he could see that he was interested in spending time with her, far beyond his 'charitable endeavours', as his mother called it.

His next words came on impulse, with no forethought whatsoever.

"How long will you be staying in London, Lady Venetia? Will you be returning to the countryside for Christmas?"

Momentarily, an odd expression crossed her face, with something of sadness, something of fear, and something of anger intermixed. It was gone almost immediately, and he questioned whether he had really seen it when she turned a bright smile to him.

"We will. It has not yet been decided exactly when we will leave London – it will depend on many things, including the weather – there is nothing worse than travelling during rain, with the roads deep in mud."

"Indeed."

In his mind, memories surfaced of muddy battlefields, and horses hock deep in clinging, sucking mud, exhausted men beside them. No road in England could ever recreate that horror, and he was thankful for that fact. He wondered, also, what that odd expression had meant – what had she been thinking of? For surely, going to one's home estate for Christmas would normally be cause for happiness, not sadness?

"In the rain, I would rather ride than travel in a carriage – I may get wet, but at least I have some choice of the path we take, and I can direct my horse away from the worst of the mud, but a carriage has only one possible path to take."

He was startled by her words, reminding him again of the fact that she rode extraordinarily well – so well that it had led to overconfidence and the fall which had resulted in her scar. Few women would choose getting wet over sitting in a comfortable carriage, yet her reasoning was sound.

"I am inclined to agree with you on that. I also have not yet decided when I will retire to the country. I have few close family, and Templewick Grange does not yet truly feel like home to me."

Those words were true, he realised as he said them – the Grange was huge, and beautiful, but it had never been his home, and making it so was difficult, for it was full of reminders of the uncle he had not particularly liked. It would, perhaps, one day feel like home, once he had wed, and had a family.

That thought startled him anew, for somehow, he had gone from being rather horrified by his need to marry and get an heir, to accepting it, even wishing for it, in some ways. How had that happened?

At that moment, Lady Thornmont went to the front of the room to call for all to be seated ready for the next performer, which put an end to any more immediate conversation. But the thoughts continued – he would, he realised, miss these conversations with Lady Venetia, when he went to the country. He had no close friends, no one to talk to but his mother, and whilst for the first months of his being Earl he had been so focussed on the estates and what he had to learn that he had barely noticed, now that he considered it, he suspected that he would feel lonely at Templewick Grange.

And at that thought, an image slipped into his mind, of Lady Venetia at Templewick Grange, in the house, but also in the stables, and riding out across the fields. It felt right, so very right that he sat there stunned. Carefully, he looked at her, sidelong, taking in the strong lines of her face as she watched the singer – who was, fortuitously, also quite talented.

Why had he imagined her at the Grange? Was he coming to care for her, more than simply as good company? He almost laughed at that – what hope would he have? What would she think, if she knew of his past? Would she turn away in disgust at his having worked as a stable master? Most women of the *ton* likely would.

*****

Venetia wished that he hadn't asked about Christmas, for that one word had reminded her of the disaster which was rapidly approaching, of the fact that she needed to make a match, to find some gentleman to marry, before their funds ran out and Christmas became a time of misery. She thought that she had prevented her feelings on the matter from showing on her face, but he had given her a slightly strange look for a moment.

What would Christmas be like, if she did find a man to marry?

And with that thought, an image slipped into her mind of herself, standing at the altar, beside this man. It made her breath catch, and it was only with great effort that she prevented a small sob from escaping her. This was a man whom she could face marrying, indeed. He was kind, amusing at times, honest and plain spoken, and he had never once done anything to suggest that he found her scarred face repulsive.

She would miss him, she realised now, once they went their separate ways to the country, miss him quite terribly, for he was the only thing which had given her hope at all.

But she could not expect him to marry her! He had never shown any sign of wishing to pay her that kind of attention, and she would not pretend to herself about such things. Just because he was kind to her, and could look at her face without flinching, did not mean that he held a tendre for her! Although... perhaps it would be pleasant if he did....

She pushed the thought away. The fact that he could look at her scar and be kind, the few times that they met out in society, did not mean that he would wish to look at it every day! She must resign herself to marrying a man who was not the sort she would have chosen, for marrying someone, and thereby not having her mother, and their tenants, starve was more important than wishing for impossible things.

The singer finished, and the third one was announced immediately, and she was soon seen to be far less talented than the first two.

Fortunately, she sang a short piece, and they were all released to the refreshments. Venetia rose, with her mother, and curtsied to Lord Templewick.

"Thank you for your conversation, my Lord."

He bowed.

"And thank you for yours. Will I see you at Lord Woolich's Ball?"

Her heart pounded in her chest.

"You will, my Lord."

"I look forward to it."

He bowed again, and to her mother also, and left them there. Venetia sighed softly, and her mother raised an eyebrow.

"Why do you sigh, Venetia? Surely the fact that he hopes to see you again is good?"

"It is, Mother, but I do not think that he is like to offer me anything other than kind friendship – although I certainly would be happy should he wish more. I cannot imagine Lord Templewick offering anything which was not honourable – unlike so many others."

Her mother sighed then, nodding in agreement.

"We must hope, then, that he begins to consider offering you more..."

*****

Weeks had passed again, weeks in which Venetia had danced with, and conversed with, the Earl of Templewick, without there ever being any indication that he might offer more. But the more time she spent with him, the more she came to feel for him, and the more she feared that she might be making her own situation worse. For what if she came to love him, which seemed entirely possible, and he did not return her affections at all?

What if she then had to marry a lecherous old man, to save them, all the while dreaming of Templewick?

They had decided that, if there were no offers – of the acceptable kind – by the end of the following week, then they would have to return to Brightwood Chase, and institute great economies, as well as selling off whatever they could to get them through the winter. As Venetia sat with Lady Hardenwell, sipping tea, relieved that there was a plan, however miserable life might end up being, Ames tapped on the parlour door.

"My Lady… there is a gentleman here, to call upon Lady Venetia."

He held the correspondence tray, and Lady Hardenwell plucked the calling card from its silver surface. Her face paled as she read it.

"Who is it, Mother?"

"Lord Blatherfort. Do you wish to admit him?"

"I…"

Before she had a chance to say more, the man in question stepped through the door, almost shoving Ames aside. They rose. Lord Blatherfort didn't bother to bow.

"No need for all of this delay! Of course she'll see me."

He waved at Ames, attempting to dismiss him. Ames ignored him. Venetia shuddered. Lady Hardenwell drew herself up, and put on her best polite society face.

"Lord Blatherfort – well, this is a surprise. Ames, please have fresh tea and an extra cup sent in."

Ames bowed, and left the room. Lord Blatherfort looked mildly annoyed that the butler had waited for Lady Hardenwell's dismissal of him, but then turned his attention back to Venetia.

"Stubborn little thing, aren't you? But I'm not a man who gives in easily. When I want something, I get it, in the end. And I want you. So much so that you've achieved something I didn't think was possible. Lady Venetia, I am here to offer for you. Well? What do you say?"

Venetia gave a half strangled, not quite a laugh, noise.

Surely he wasn't serious? But it seemed that he was. He was watching her, waiting for her reaction, seemingly expecting delight. All she felt was revulsion. The thought of marrying a man like this, of going to his bed, made her feel physically ill.

The silence stretched, and he began to look irritated, tapping his fingers on his knee.

There was another tap at the door, and Rosie entered with a new tea tray. She set it down in front of Lady Hardenwell, and left the room, but not without a sidelong questioning look at Venetia.

Lady Hardenwell poured, and handed Lord Blatherfort a cup. He appeared annoyed, and for a moment, Venetia thought he might reject the tea. But he gave her a rather grim smile, accepted the cup, and sipped politely. All of this gave her, and her mother, time to consider what to say.

She could not laugh in the man's face, could not afford to have him speak badly of them in society, yet she could not, simply could not, countenance the idea of marrying him. Starvation would be better. She sipped her own tea as a pool of icy fear, which the tea did nothing to warm, settled in her stomach. Then, with a clink which startled her, Lady Hardenwell set her own cup down on the side table.

"Lord Blatherfort, this comes as somewhat of a surprise, given the... suggestions... which you have made to Lady Venetia a number of times before. Might I enquire about the... motivation... for your change of heart on this matter?"

Lord Blatherfort looked, for a moment, ready to explode. He was obviously not used to a woman questioning or challenging him in any way.

"I do not see why I need to explain myself to you. Surely the generosity of my willingness to marry your daughter is enough?"

"It is not. Lady Venetia's father is dead. I am her guardian – and discussion of marriage and the like which might normally have happened with her father will happen with me."

Venetia wanted to cheer her mother on. The more she saw of this man, the more she knew that marrying him would be a terrible mistake. But she sat quietly, watching. It seemed that he had come here expecting easy acquiescence – and now was unsure how to respond.

"If you must know, I have changed what I am willing to offer for one reason only. News has just reached me that my son, who has been travelling in India, was carried off by one of those dreadful tropical diseases, quite some months ago. Only one wife of the three I've had managed to bear me a child who lived, and now he is gone. To be blunt, I now lack an heir. I need a young healthy wife to breed me another one, as soon as possible. Breeding does not require beauty, but a healthy strong body is of assistance. As Lady Venetia is unlikely to get any other offers, this seemed a good solution for both of us."

Venetia was, by the end of that little speech, positively shaking with fury. There he was, discussing her as if she was a cow, or a brood mare, not a person. Her mother was also furious, although only someone who knew her well would recognise the signs. She had stilled, and her face was pale, with a little heightened colour high on her cheeks, and she shook – infinitesimally, but it was there.

"I see. And what are your expectations with respect to money? Lady Venetia's dowry is not large, but I would expect a marriage contract which would provide well for her future, with a suitable widow's jointure, for example. Have you all of the details of such things laid out?"

Lord Blatherfort swallowed heavily.

"I have not – it seemed unnecessary to bother which such detail now, when she will get no other offers."

"Then you should not have offered. I suggest that you consider these things, and return here tomorrow, so that we might provide you with her answer – and even then, should the answer be yes, all of the financial matters will need to be in order."

"You, madam, are ungrateful, and unsuitably arrogant for a woman. But as I feel some urgency on this matter. I will do as you say."

With that, he set his cup down and simply left, without even a bow. Neither of them moved until they heard the front door close behind him.

"Mother..."

Lady Hardenwell laughed, waving a hand at Venetia.

"Do not fear, my darling, I would never, never suggest that you accept a man like that. I just needed a way to make him perhaps reconsider, and to get him out of the house now, so that we can plan. A direct refusal now would have produced anger – this way is better. Tomorrow, he will be more prepared to be told no."

Venetia half collapsed into her chair, relief filling her.

"I could not..." she shuddered, shaking her head, "starvation would be better than that!"

"Indeed, it would. We shall see what happens tomorrow – but, no matter what, you will not be marrying Lord Blatherfort. I shudder to think what his three previous wives went through, if he only managed one living child between them. I sincerely hoped that you might receive a better offer – but we will survive, somehow, regardless."

*****

The following evening, after a harrowing day during which Lord Blatherfort, upon finding himself rejected, insulted them in language worthy of a sailor, Venetia and her mother stepped into the ballroom nervously, waiting to see what word of anything might have reached the gossips. They were welcomed by the usual group of wallflowers and their mothers, but the conversation was not focussed on Lord Blatherfort at all.

"Lady Hardenwell, Lady Venetia! There is wonderful news! Lord Merringbar has offered for my Amelia! And she has accepted. They are to marry by license next week, so that they can travel for their wedding trip before the roads are too bad."

Venetia forced herself to smile, even while her heart sank entirely. Lord Merringbar was older, but quite good looking, and seemed a reasonable man. Miss Amelia Hanson was lucky, and Venetia could see at a glance that all of the other girls positively burned with envy.

"How wonderful for you. My congratulations."

What else could she say? At least this conversation was better than having Lord Blatherfort's offer for her as the subject of the day.

Chapter Ten

Venetia stayed to the edges of the excited conversation around Miss Hanson, unable to raise the required enthusiasm to be part of it. She was staring blankly across the room to where the acknowledged beauties danced with the most handsome admirers, desperately wishing that she could turn back time, that she could choose not to take that jump, that she could be one of those girls, rather than the outcast that she had become.

It was pointless wishing, for nothing could be changed, but that did not stop her wishing it, regardless.

"Dreaming of what might have been?"

The voice was soft, barely a whisper, and from so close to her ear that she could feel his breath on her skin. A quiver ran through her, her heart raced, and her mouth went suddenly dry. She did not turn, however, but simply smiled, knowing who it was, immediately. Her tongue darted out to moisten her lips before she spoke, her whisper just as low as his.

"Indeed. Although perhaps with a better understanding of what I actually wish for, now, than I would ever have had before."

She heard his sharp intake of breath, and knew, with an odd pang in her heart, that he understood what she meant.

How was it that this man could so easily reach the truth of her, could understand her, and not only accept, but actually seek her blunt and baldly honest statements, rather than expecting bland platitudes? And, even more importantly, why did she feel comfortable with that, why did she trust him to hold her secrets close, rather than spreading gossip? For she did trust him, she had come to realise, in a way that she did not trust any other man she'd met.

"Is that pragmatism I hear? Surely, an unusual quality to find in a young Lady."

"Having one's choices severely restricted commonly leads to the development of pragmatism."

He was silent, after another sharp intake of breath. She waited a moment, steadying herself, then turned, to find him standing very close indeed. Her eyes met his, and the world went still and silent around her as their brown depths drew her in. There was peace in that sensation, but danger as well – oh so much danger, for if she allowed herself to fall into those depths, she could fall forever, could be caught up in feelings which she could not permit herself to have.

She forced herself to break that eye contact – which led to her eyes considering the rest of his handsome face – and that was almost as bad! She drew a ragged breath.

"Lady Venetia, might I hope for a dance?"

She laughed then, with only a little of bitterness in it.

"You need not hope, my Lord, for you know full well that the availability of a dance is guaranteed, or you would not have found me here, dreaming."

"Then, if you will allow it, I will take full advantage of that fact."

"I will allow it, gladly."

"I shall keep you company here, until the next dance is about to begin." He angled his head towards the cluster of women nearby. "Has something happened to cause this scene of excitement?"

Venetia sighed softly, and he raised an eyebrow enquiringly.

"Miss Amelia Hanson has become betrothed to Lord Merringbar. She is lucky, for he seems a decent man, and all of the other girls are excited for her – and dreadfully envious."

"Ah, I see. Let us speak of other things, then. When we spoke at the musicale, neither of us had yet decided when we might be leaving London – that, on my part at least, has now changed. I do not feel that I can achieve much more in London – not until the spring. I am therefore going to take myself back to Templewick Grange, leaving in a few days' time. I want to be certain that the tenants are all well set up for the colder weather, while I still have time to arrange repairs to their cottages if required."

Venetia turned her head away for a moment, struck with a pang of sorrow at the thought of not seeing him, of having his company taken from her so soon.

"We will also be leaving London within the week. It has become obvious that I am unlikely to make a match at present, so we will go home for the winter, and return to London in March. Perhaps, by then..."

A tightness passed across his face, fleetingly, and she wondered what had caused it, but he said nothing in response. She was almost certain, however, that he had heard the unspoken end to her sentence *'by then, my scar may have faded...'*.

The current dance ended, and he offered his arm, ready to lead her to the dance floor as soon as the current dancers moved off. She took it, and soon they were dancing, letting most conversation drop in favour of simply enjoying themselves, of ignoring all things serious for some time. If only she could forget her troubles entirely...

*****

In the carriage on the way home, Morgan was silent.

His mother, uncharacteristically, left it at that, and he immersed himself in his thoughts. Thoughts of his own feelings, which disturbed him.

When Lady Venetia had spoken of making a match, something sharp had twisted inside him – yet he had always known that she was hoping for such a thing. Nonetheless, he found that he did not like the idea of her marrying any of the gentlemen who might be a possibility. She deserved far better than lechers and wastrels!

The intensity of his response surprised him – she was not his to worry about, indeed, she deserved a better man than him, for she needed someone who was stainless in the eyes of society, who had no unsuitable history to be discovered. He shook his head – was he truly considering her as if there might be something between them? Did he want there to be?

He did not know the answers to those questions, but the fact that he even asked them of himself troubled him.

Perhaps it was best if he left these thoughts alone, and focussed more on the things he needed to resolve in his own life, rather than wishing to affect someone else!

But still, came the small voice in his mind, *there is something between you – there has been, from the first moment that your eyes met hers, as she lay there in blood spattered confusion.*

*****

The week had passed quickly, with no further proposals, and, fortunately, without there being any gossip about her refusal of Lord Blatherfort. She suspected that he wished, as much as she did, for it not to become known. After all, to be refused by the woman least likely to receive another offer was something which could easily have brought him significant mockery.

They had packed up and left Hardenwell House with no sadness at the departure – it was no longer a home to them, and removing themselves from Lord Jasper's proximity was most welcome. The journey had gone well, with no rain, and little mud on the roads, much to their relief. But now, two days later, as they sat in the small office at Brightwood Grange, the estate ledgers open in front of them, Venetia almost wished she was back in London.

She missed being able to go about and enjoy herself – as much as was possible, since her scar – and she missed, most of all, her conversations and dances with Lord Templewick. She missed him, in a way that she had never missed anyone before. It was rather disconcerting, and she was annoyed with herself – he had given no indication of hoping for anything more than friendship, so why did she still dream of him, still hope...

She shook her head, and turned her attention back to the ledgers.

"Mother, is this as bad as I think it is?"

Lady Hardenwell nodded.

"It is indeed bad. This year's crops have not brought in as much income as we had hoped, for we had to keep enough back for next year's seed, as well as to feed the tenants, and the horses, through the winter. I will need to look at everything over the next two weeks, and discover where we might make economies, and what we might sell – at the moment, I do not believe that we have funds to take us past early January."

"Is there anything that I can do to help?"

Her mother looked at her with a most serious expression.

"Pray for a miracle – because I think that we will need one."

*****

Templewick was quiet. The house seemed huge around them, and felt empty.

While they had been in London, the servants had moved all that remained of his uncle's, and his family's, personal possessions into one of the least used guest suites, and begun the refurbishment of a number of rooms. It no longer felt like his uncle's home, but it did not yet feel like his own.

It was, as he had suspected it would be, a lonely place. He might not have found many of the gentlemen in London particularly convivial, but they had been company, and there had been those conversations with Lady Venetia. He found himself thinking of her frequently, missing her, in a way that he had not expected to.

For the weeks since returning, he'd thrown himself into the process of the refurbishments, into assessing and dealing with the remaining personal effects of his uncle, and into ensuring that the estates were ready for winter, but, all of the time, thoughts of Lady Venetia slipped into his quieter moments.

And those thoughts showed him, quite clearly, just how much he liked her.

Perhaps he should have done more, spent more time with her? The thought appealed, now that it was too late. He was ashamed to admit to himself that his fear of the gossips had kept him from displaying the true interest which he felt in her. That truth shocked him, for he had been many things, but not ever a coward – until now.

He did not know what to do about it, but the knowledge of it, the fact that he had lost the opportunity to spend time with her, because of his own hesitations, grated. It worried away at him, as if demanding that he do something to redress that wrong. He stared into the fire, oblivious to his surroundings, his mind full of Lady Venetia's face, and the words she'd said when he'd last seen her – about finding a match.

As the words had then, the memory of them sent a sharp pang through his heart. He could not imagine any man of the *ton* who might offer for her, who would actually be worthy of her.

"Morgan? Did you hear me?"

His mother's voice broke through his thoughts.

He suspected that she'd been speaking to him for some minutes.

"I... didn't. I'm sorry."

She sighed.

"What were you thinking about? You've been very pensive since we came back from London – is something wrong? Or... are you pining for something... or someone... left behind in London?"

Startled, he turned and met her eyes.

"No... I... well..."

She laughed, shaking her head.

"I'll take that to mean that yes, there is someone you miss, and that you don't know what to do about it."

He sighed – she'd always been good at understanding his moods, and the years he'd been away hadn't changed that.

"You're right."

She nodded, smiling.

"Good – because I have some ideas about what to do. Tell me a little of your thoughts if you will, and then I'll tell you what I want to suggest."

*****

"If we keep just the one carriage, and just the strongest pair to pull it, plus a riding horse each, we should realise a decent sum. The brood mares are valuable, and the stallion will bring a good price, even if he is getting a bit old now. After that, we'll be down to selling more of the paintings and some of the silverware, and as a last resort, reducing staff, but selling the horses and carriages should get us through to March if they sell well. I've sent letters to those we've sold horses to before, and given them first options."

Venetia sipped her tea, considering her mother's words. Her mind went back to London, to the hopes she'd nurtured, the hopes which revolved around Lord Templewick. She'd obviously been a complete fool. But she still dreamed about him, still wished for more.

When her mother spoke of needing a miracle, in Venetia's mind, the miracle was presented in the form of one particular Earl. Those thoughts were so foolish that she nearly laughed at herself, but knowing that did not banish them.

"Have any of them responded?"

"It's only been a week since I sent them – but yes, one has responded so far – Lord Crosswood is sending a man to assess the horses we have on offer, and potentially purchase on the spot. If we are lucky, he will arrive today, or perhaps tomorrow."

Lord Crosswood! Wasn't he the one whose man had sewn up her face?

"Wasn't Lord Crosswood the one whose horse was collected the day of my fall?"

Her mother nodded, her expression holding sadness.

"He was – it was his man who did such tidy work on your face. Perhaps it will be the same man who comes this time?"

A shiver ran through Venetia at the thought – but she knew, in the same instant, that it would not be the same man. For she felt more and more certain that the man who had worked on her face was the same man who was now the Earl of Templewick. It was improbable, and she could not imagine how it could be true, and yet she felt that it was, with a deep inner certainty. Not that she could ever have asked him – that would have been unforgivably intrusive, and insulting, should it not be the same person.

"Perhaps..." It was at that exact moment that a knock came upon the front door. They looked at each other, and Venetia gave a half choked off laugh. "Have we summoned him with our words?"

"We shall see in a moment, shan't we?"

They listened as the butler opened the door, and a few moments later, there was a tap on the parlour door.

"Enter."

The door opened.

"My Lady, Mr Holley has come from Lord Crosswood – about the horses."

They rose, and the man bowed, a little awkwardly, cap in hand. Venetia studied him carefully, but she knew, from her first glance, that this was a different man. She glanced at her mother, whose momentary expression showed that she agreed with that assessment.

"I am pleased to see you, Mr Holley. I will summon our groom, and he can show you the mares we are selling. Then, if you come back to the house, we can sit down in the office and discuss prices – assuming that you decide than some of them will suit Lord Crosswood."

"Thank you, Lady Hardenwell."

She turned to their butler.

"Please summon the groom." He nodded, and left the room. She turned back to Mr Holley. "Mr Holley, I do believe that a different man came, last time that we sold a mare to Lord Crosswood – I had thought to perhaps see the same man again."

Mr Holley shifted his feet, obviously far less comfortable in the parlour than he would be in the stables.

"Yes, my Lady. Mr Follett moved on from Lord Crosswood's employ not long after he came here. He had a most unexpected inheritance – I'm told he's now an Earl, after the previous Earl and his whole family were taken off by the cholera! We were all pleased for him – he was a good man to work with – and his good fortune – not the loss of his relatives, mind, but the inheritance - was also mine, as I went from Head Groom to Stablemaster as a result. He spoke well of the quality of your horses, my Lady, so I'm hoping that we can do business today."

"I hope so too."

Their groom appeared in the doorway.

"You sent for me, my Lady?"

Venetia barely heard the conversation as her mother directed their groom to show Mr Holley the correct horses, and to then bring him back to the house, where some refreshments would be provided whilst they discussed the details of whatever purchases were to be made. Her attention was all to her thoughts.

She dropped back into her chair, and her fingers went to the scar, tracing the fine bumps which were slowly fading to a softer pink.

What Mr Holley had said appeared to confirm her suspicions – for his story of the unexpected Earl aligned very closely with what she knew about the Earl of Templewick. Which meant that the man who had sewn up her face, the man she had dreamed about ever since, was one and the same as the Earl of Templewick – who also filled her dreams.

But if that was the case, why had he never mentioned it?

Chapter Eleven

As the days went by, Morgan felt more and more out of sorts. Christmas was approaching, yet he could not look forward to it in any way. Unless he managed to make something change, it would be lonely and uninspiring. To make things worse, his desire to see Lady Venetia only grew with time, rather than decreasing – it was like an itch he couldn't scratch, and he mentally castigated himself regularly for having been such a fool as to not spend more time with her when he could have. And especially for not having shown her that he found her interesting – for he did, he now knew, and in ways that related to far more than conversation.

But what could he do to provide company and entertainment for Christmas? He had few relatives now, and those were distant, his mother's relatives were people he hardly knew, who had been uninterested in him – but now that he was Earl, that had probably changed. Still, he doubted that they would be good company...

Perhaps some of the people he had met in London?

He wasn't sure about that idea at all, so he pushed the thoughts aside, and went back to concentrating on the state of his estates, and what must be done before snow set in. His uncle had not been particularly generous with his tenants, but at least his estate manager had not outright mistreated them, so there was necessary maintenance to do, but nothing disastrous.

*****

Lord Crosswood's man had bought all four brood mares for his master, but not the stallion. It wasn't enough, but it was a start – enough, Venetia's mother thought, to get them through to Twelfth Night, but not much further. Lady Hardenwell had sent out letters to various people, seeking a buyer for the large travelling coach, and the pair of larger horses to pull it, but as yet, they'd had no interest from anyone.

The mail had just been brought in for the day, after one of the footmen had been to the village to collect it and some supplies for the kitchen. Venetia watched as Lady Hardenwell opened it, wishing with all her might that one of those letters might be someone interested in the coach. When all were opened, Lady Hardenwell set them down on the side table with a sigh.

"Nothing of use, Mother?"

"Nothing. Some gossip from one of my friends in London, a brief note from your uncle hoping that our stay at Hardenwell House went well, our monthly invoice from the village store, and a note from Lord Crosswood, letting us know that the mares arrived in good order, and that he is delighted with them. But nothing which might bring us any income, I am afraid."

Venetia's heart dropped. Things were beginning to look very bleak.

"Surely we will find a solution soon."

"I do not have any great confidence about that, I am sorry to say. But we must keep trying – perhaps there will be some Christmas Balls in the district, and opportunities for you to meet gentlemen there?"

"Perhaps."

Venetia tried to smile, but she feared it was not a convincing expression. Her mind went back over their weeks in London – was there any more that she could have done, to make a suitable match? Surely she could have encouraged Lord Templewick more?

But she shook her head at that thought – he had offered nothing more than kind friendship – and how could she have encouraged more, when she valued that friendship so much? She could not have, not without doing something which was against her nature.

She thought over all of the men who had offered her anything – but only Lord Blatherfort and two others had offered marriage, and the other two were just as repulsive as Blatherfort – well, perhaps not quite as much, but very close. Could she, if it came to it, bear to accept one of them? A shudder of horror ran through her at the thought, but she forced herself to look at the idea. Would it not be better than starving? Than reaching the point where they lost everything?

Perhaps it would. But she could not face that idea yet. If her mother thought that they had funds enough to get to Twelfth Night, then she would give herself that long, before doing anything rash.

And she would pray for a miracle to come to save them, every single day. Prayers in which she was sure that the miracle of her imagination would look like Lord Templewick.

*****

"I've been thinking about what you told me – about feeling lonely and rather isolated here. And about what you didn't say, about the sort of company you're missing."

Morgan lifted his head from his book and met his mother's eyes. He wasn't sure exactly what she meant, but he had his suspicions.

"And... I take it that you have come to some conclusions?"

She smiled.

"Oh yes, I most definitely have."

Those words left him with the distinct feeling that, whatever that conclusion was, he was going to be doomed to act upon it.

"I see. Will I like these conclusions?"

She laughed then, and shook her head a little.

"I am not sure – perhaps not until you get used to the idea."

Despite himself, he was intrigued.

"If that is the case, then you had best inform me of it, forthwith, so that I can begin to adjust to whatever it is that you are about to convince me to do."

"Convince you? Surely you will go along with my suggestions, just to please me, as any good son would do for his mother?"

There was laughter in her voice, and he grinned at her.

"I reserve the right to resist, at least a little."

She sighed dramatically, and tried to look put upon, but spoiled it by losing the battle against laughter. A few minutes passed before she contained her mirth, then she spoke, with a more serious tone.

"As to the loneliness, it seems obvious to me that the best solution is to arrange company. But as to the things you did not speak about, the only solution for that is to arrange the company of specific people… "

Internally, he flinched. He was quite sure that those words meant that she had detected his feelings about Lady Venetia. He did not know how, but she had always been most astute, so he must have given himself away, somehow.

"So far that sounds sensible – although I don't quite see how 'arranging company' can easily be done?"

"There is one very simple solution. You must hold a house party - perhaps a week or so before Christmas – and invite those people you found most convivial in London – male and female. The women will obviously need to come with parents or chaperones, but I am sure that they will be glad to attend. And you can invite the members of the aristocracy and the landed gentry who live not too far distant – they are sure to be curious about you, and attend. This house is enormous, so space to accommodate them shouldn't be a problem."

Morgan swallowed, hard. The thought of having his home invaded in such a way was not, at first, appealing – which was no doubt the reaction she'd expected from him. So before he spoke, he considered the idea carefully. If it was only for a week, surely he could bear it that long? And it would provide company, as well as allowing him to get to know various people better. And… the concept of a house party attended by women, as well as gentlemen, did hold appeal.

Yes, said his thoughts, *especially if Lady Venetia is one of those women.*

He met his mother's expectant gaze, and smiled.

"I think, perhaps, that is actually a good idea." She looked startled, and he smiled, pleased to see that reaction. "Mind you, I have absolutely no concept of how to organise such a thing, so you would need to assist – a lot."

She waved a hand.

"Of course. That won't be a problem, and the staff here know how to do everything that is required, as well. All that you will have to do is decide upon the guest list, and write the actual invitations."

He nodded, his mind turning over rapidly, suddenly full of possibilities. He still wasn't used to having the number of staff that they had now, nor was he used to having the financial resources which the Earldom provided. Perhaps this would not be so difficult as he'd first thought it might be.

"I believe that I can manage that. Although… deciding on a guest list may well tax me extremely. Leave me to think about that, please. But if you could set everything else in motion, with the staff and the like, I would be most grateful."

"I can do that, most decidedly. I must say, I think that is the easiest that you have ever agreed to one of my suggestions – either I am getting better at this, or you are mellowing as you age!"

Morgan snorted with laughter.

"As I age? I don't think I'm quite doddering yet!"

*****

"Not quite what I'm looking for, my Lady, I'm sorry."

"Of course, my Lord. If you know of anyone else who might be interested, do please let them know."

The man bowed.

"I will, be assured. Good day to you, Lady Hardenwell."

He turned and left, and Venetia came down the steps to where her mother stood on the forecourt, watching the gentleman ride away. She slipped an arm around her mother and hugged her gently.

"Someone will want to buy it, eventually, I am sure. It is a very nice carriage..."

Lady Hardenwell sighed.

"I certainly hope so. Come, let us go inside and have some tea whilst we consider our next moves."

They went in, and said nothing more until they each had a cup of tea in hand.

"Mother, are we sure that there is nothing else we can sell?"

"Nothing – unless, that is, you want to start selling the furniture We've already sold the few paintings which were worth anything."

Venetia sighed, sadness and fear filling her.

"There must be something we can do..."

"Nothing that I have been able to think of. And I've tried my hardest..."

The image rose in Venetia's mind of the least offensive of the three men who had suggested marriage.

She swallowed – it was time to at least talk to her mother about that possibility.

"I... I could always write to Lord Peterley. He, whilst old, and a lecher, was the least horrible of those who seemed willing to marry me. I suppose that marriage to him would be better than us starving, and losing everything... And, to be horribly pragmatic, he is also the oldest of them – I believe he is well into his eighties, even if he seems sprightly. Surely that means that I would not have to suffer the marriage for too many years?"

Lady Hardenwell shuddered, so strongly that she nearly dropped her cup.

"No! Don't even consider it – we will find a way, somehow, that doesn't involve you giving yourself to someone like that. Anyway – he's not especially wealthy, and I have no idea whether he would even be willing to assist me – men that old can get obnoxious and stubborn."

"If you're sure... But I am practical about this – if Twelfth Night comes, and what funds we have are near gone, then we must consider this idea again – even though it is the last thing I want to do."

Lady Hardenwell nodded slowly.

"You are right, much though I desperately wish you weren't. Let us pray that we are granted a miracle before Christmas."

*****

"My potential guest list is rather lamentably short, Mother. Perhaps you can help me add to it?"

His mother looked up from her embroidery with a smile.

"Of course – show me what you have so far."

Morgan passed her the sheet of paper on which he had noted the names of people he thought he could bear to have at a house party.

Most of the men were tolerable, although he wasn't sure that he truly liked many of them. As for ladies, the only ones on that list at this point were Lady Venetia and Lady Hardenwell.

"Hmm, I see what you mean. There are probably enough young gentlemen here, but the list of ladies needs definite expansion – although I do approve of what you have so far."

There was amusement in her voice, and Morgan almost squirmed on his seat, knowing full well that she realised that he was interested in Lady Venetia.

"Kind of you... but who else can I invite? I don't know many of the young women well – you most likely know their mothers, which is why I am asking you."

She nodded, and rose, going to the small escritoire which sat in the corner of the large parlour. She brought out a pen and the ink pot from its storage, and set about adding names to the paper. After a moment, she looked up at him.

"Morgan, I could just choose well known young women - there are many out this year who would be suitable, although I suspect you'd find most of them rather dull. But I have an idea. In the same way that you chose to converse and dance with the wallflowers, the ones who were not generally noticed, perhaps you should continue that kindness by inviting those young women to your house party. In a closed environment for a week, with none of the acknowledged beauties present, surely some of them will manage to draw the attention of the better young men?"

He considered it for a moment, and was sure, as he did, that it was a stroke of genius. Whilst he had not found most of the wallflowers especially appealing, they had all been far more genuine people than the feted beauties.

"Indeed, I like that idea, Mother. If you know the names and direction for the ladies and their families, let us certainly add them to the list. If we make the numbers of younger men and women somewhat equal, then no one should lack for conversation and company."

She spent a few minutes writing, adding names to the list, then looked up at him.

"I know most of them, and can obtain the direction of the others through people I do know. Let us draft a suitable invitation, and then you can write it out for each one."

"Just one thing, before that – a few of the gentlemen I have on that list I do not know particularly well, and I wondered if you thought I had chosen the right sort of people?"

She looked at the list again, a tiny frown appearing on her face as she thought carefully, then shook her head.

"In truth, I cannot give you a precise answer, but all of those you have listed here are of good families, and I do not recall having heard any negative gossip about them. I can see no reason to specifically exclude any of these people, so I would say that we should invite them, and see how things go."

*****

It was barely three weeks to Christmas, and still, no one had bought the carriage. Venetia felt more afraid every day, that she would, in the end, have to consider marrying Lord Peterley. Each day, they waited eagerly for the footman to return from the village with the mail, and each day they had been disappointed by polite replies expressing a complete lack of interest in buying. Still, Venetia was determined to hope.

There was a tap at the parlour door.

"Enter."

The footman came in, and proffered the correspondence tray. Venetia held her breath as her mother lifted the three letters from the silver tray, praying that this time there would be something of use to them.

The footman left the room, and Lady Hardenwell looked at each letter, attempting to discern who had sent them. She frowned, a puzzled look on her face, and set one aside, then went about breaking the seals on the other two.

"Lord Winthrop has decided against buying the stallion. And Lord Sharmont has decided against the carriage."

"Oh no! I thought that Lord Winthrop was rather keen on the stallion! But – what of the third letter? Why did you set it aside?"

Lady Hardenwell dropped the two opened letters onto the small table beside her, and lifted the third, unopened one. She studied it again for a moment, then gave a small shrug, and broke the seal.

"I had set it aside because I did not recognise the writing. Let me read it."

She unfolded the letter, and read, her eyes widening as she did, and a small gasp escaped her.

"What is it? Is it something good?"

Without a word, her mother handed the letter to Venetia.

> *The Earl of Templewick would be pleased to have the company of Lady Hardenwell and Lady Venetia Chater for a Christmas House Party, to be held at Templewick Grange for the last full week before Christmas.*
>
> *The party will be attended by a select group of the aristocracy, and some of the more important people who live close to Templewick. I look forward to seeing you amongst the attendees.*
>
> *Please advise if you will attend as soon as possible, so that all arrangements can be made.*
>
> *Yrs.*
>
> *Templewick.*

Chapter Twelve

In the parlour of a respectable home, not too far from Hardenwell House in London, Lord Jasper Chater sat with Richard, Viscount Wilborough, who he classed as a friend. As much, that was, as Jasper regarded anyone as a friend – mostly, Jasper saw people as useful, or not. Lord Wilborough was generally well respected, and knew all of the 'right people' but was also not averse to an evening of gambling – or to occasionally lending his friends money.

They each held a glass of brandy, even though it was not quite evening yet, and had been discussing the coming Christmas season, and what entertainments it might bring, when a tap at the door interrupted their musings. Wilborough raised an eyebrow, seeming startled.

"Enter."

The butler came in, carrying a tray.

"My Lord, a letter has just arrived for you."

He held out the tray, and Wilborough lifted the letter from it, waving the butler away. When he just looked at it with a frown, Jasper, impatient as always, spoke.

"Well? Are you going to open it? Or just sit there and stare at it as if it might bite?"

Wilborough laughed, shaking his head, and broke the seal. He read for a moment, then looked up with a grin on his face.

"Well now, this seems to solve our problem of what to do for entertainment – at least for the week or so before Christmas, anyway."

"It does? How? What is it?"

Wilborough waved the paper.

"This, my friend, is an invitation to a house party at Templewick Grange. The way it reads, it could be a respectable party, or a not so respectable party – but Templewick seems a decent enough man, so I think that we should go. I'm sure he won't mind me bringing a friend, and if it turns out to be dull, we can always leave. I'll send off an acceptance, and tell him I'm bringing a friend."

Jasper rubbed his hands together.

"That sounds excellent. And if it's dull, I am sure that we can find ways to liven it up, eh?"

They both laughed and lifted their glasses in a toast.

"To Christmas entertainment."

*****

"I will write an acceptance immediately! This is the miracle we have been praying for, surely. Templewick Grange is not too far to travel, especially as, so far, there has been no snow, and not too much rain, so that the roads should be passable."

Lady Hardenwell rose, and went to the escritoire in the corner of the parlour, with the invitation in hand. Venetia was still stunned by the fact that the invitation existed – not only was it another chance to meet people, and to potentially find a man she could marry, but it was a chance provided by the one man she actually found interesting. Did this invitation mean that, perhaps, he found her interesting too? Or was it just courtesy?

"Do you think that he chose to invite us for a specific reason?"

Lady Hardenwell looked up with a smile.

"We can hope so – are you wishing that this is because he likes you more than he had indicated before? Or simply because you like him?"

Venetia felt her face flush.

"I do, indeed, like him – but that is of no import unless he likes me far more than the friendship he has offered so far would indicate. Which doesn't mean that I am without hope. There must be a reason that he chose to invite us, after all."

"That's very true. This house party is little more than a week away now – you'd best start planning what clothes to take, to look your best." She paused, and looked at Venetia closely. "At least your scar has faded a lot in the weeks since we returned from London – perhaps people will be less judgemental now."

Venetia swallowed a sudden urge to tears.

"I certainly hope so. I will leave you to write and send our acceptance, and I'll go and start preparing my things right now."

*****

Acceptances had begun to arrive, and the fact that he would soon have a house full of near strangers to cater for had suddenly taken on a reality which it had not held before.

The amount of organisation required was huge – massive amounts of food, extra staff, the cleaning and airing of a whole wing of Templewick Grange, the similar preparation of stables and space in the coach house – that was just the beginning. His mother had taken to the whole process with a kind of ferocious joy which he envied, and was utterly grateful for as well.

Quite how he would keep all of these people entertained, he wasn't sure.

He stared at the list in front of him, and gave a low groan of frustration. Once one exhausted the completely obvious, like hunting, and rides around the grounds, and a ball or celebratory dinner one evening, it became harder and harder to think up entertainments which might amuse adults. Children would have been far easier.

There were silly indoor games, like charades, and less silly ones, like cards. There were outdoor games and activities, like archery – assuming the required equipment actually existed somewhere in the store rooms or attics – he had set a number of footmen the task of exploring to look for such things. There were things like asking the guests to collaborate on the production of a small play, or perhaps a poetry reading would be easier. Most of the ideas made him shudder – he, personally, would not want to indulge in such activities, so why should he expect other people to do so?

But... his mother had assured him that they would expect such things.

He went back to the list, praying that things would be simplified by the footmen discovering the equipment for certain activities, and not others, thus removing choice. His thoughts however, refused to stay on innocuous entertainments.

Instead, the image of Lady Venetia rose in his mind, and he smiled, dreaming of the moment when he would see her again – for see her he would, as the acceptance from her mother, for both of them, had arrived this morning. This time, he would not be such a fool – he would, assuming she seemed likely to be receptive, make certain that she knew of his interest in her.

But would she be interested in him? Had he misread the way she had acted towards him, in London? He did not think so...

He forced himself to turn back to the numerous lists on his desk – it was a time for action, not for dreaming – dreaming could come later.

*****

Half of the guests had already arrived – mainly the gentlemen, with the ladies expected over the next two days. Morgan went down to the foyer, having just heard the sound of carriage wheels on the gravel – he had no idea who would arrive next, but he liked to greet his guests personally.

Pelham, the butler, opened the front door as Morgan reached the first-floor landing, and paused to watch. The first man through the door was Lord Wilborough – a decent enough seeming chap, although somewhat prone to gambling, from what Morgan had heard. The second man, however, was not a man that Morgan recognised.

He frowned, a faint memory surfacing of his mother saying that one man had said he was bringing a friend, and hurried down the last flight of steps. The two men turned, having just handed their hats and coats to Pelham.

“Good Day, gentlemen. Welcome to my home. Wilborough, I don’t believe I’ve met your friend?”

Lord Wilborough grinned, and waved a hand at the other man.

“This is Lord Jasper Chater – Chater, this is Lord Templewick.”

It was, as introductions went, about the most informal he’d ever been faced with. He raised an eyebrow at Wilborough, and turned to face Lord Jasper.

“Lord Jasper – I hope that you will enjoy your stay. Pelham here will have a footman show you to your rooms, and we’ll have your luggage brought up. After you’ve refreshed yourselves, ask a footman to show you to the large parlour – everyone has just begun to gather for drinks, and dinner will be at seven.”

Lord Jasper smiled – and Morgan clenched his teeth – the man did not look pleasant – rather, he appeared arrogant and almost sneering.

“Oh, I’m quite certain that I’ll enjoy myself, Templewick. If things are dull, there are always ways to liven house parties up.”

He gave a bow, and turned to go with Wilborough, following the waiting footman. Morgan watched them walk away, then met Pelham’s eyes.

"That one will bear watching, I think, if you would advise the staff."

"Indeed, my Lord. I will do so."

Morgan turned, and went in search of his mother, intent on asking her what she knew of this Lord Jasper.

*****

It was close on what might normally be dinner time when their carriage finally drew up before the imposing house which was Templewick Grange. Venetia, upon stepping out of the carriage and looking up at the enormous building, found herself overwhelmed, and nervous as a result.

Which was ridiculous – she had coped with *ton* events in London, all whilst being mocked and scorned – why should she feel nervous about a country house party?

She took a deep breath, and followed her mother up the steps, to where a butler was waiting at the open door. They gave him their names, and as he went to speak, Venetia's attention was caught by movement, and she looked past the butler to the elegant staircase which dominated the large foyer. The staircase which Lord Templewick was, at that very moment, descending.

Her mouth was suddenly dry, and her heart ran twice as fast as usual. He was, if that was possible, even more handsome than she had remembered. In that instant, she wanted him to care for her, more than she had ever wanted anything in her life before. His eyes met hers, and he smiled – a genuine, welcoming smile, with no hint of disgust at the existence of her scar. Something inside her unfurled, like fluttering wings.

He reached the bottom of the stairs, and came to them immediately.

"Lady Hardenwell, Lady Venetia, I am so glad that you could come – the party will be all the better for your company."

He bowed, and both she and her mother curtsied.

"We are very happy to be here, my Lord, for Christmas was most likely to be very quiet, and now you have given us this opportunity for convivial company!"

Her mother's voice was warm, and Venetia felt sure that Lord Templewick knew what she meant by 'very quiet' but was far too polite to comment. Instead, he gave that delightful smile again.

"I am sure that you must be tired after your journey," he waved a maid forward, from where she stood, waiting, "Anna will show you to your rooms, and make sure that your maid and your luggage find their way to you as quickly as possible. Once you have freshened up, everyone who has arrived so far can be found in the large parlour. Dinner is scheduled for an hour from now, so your arrival was timed perfectly."

"Thank you for your consideration. We will join you in the parlour soon."

With that, they followed the maid, as Lord Templewick turned his attention to another new arrival, whose carriage had, at that moment, drawn up outside.

The rooms they had been allocated were large, and shared a small sitting room, and each had a dressing room, plus there was a small room off one dressing room for Molly. Overall, it was most satisfactory, and, as Lady Hardenwell remarked, a stark contrast to the rooms they had first been offered at Hardenwell House when they had gone to London.

Even more so was the service they received – they were offered a warm bath, should they wish it, and the assistance of another maid if needed. Venetia had thought well of Lord Templewick before, but now, her opinion of him was further enhanced.

Molly unpacked their clothes – at least enough for them to change out of their travelling clothes, and into something more appropriate for dinner.

"Does this suit, Mother?"

"It does – and with just a touch of face powder, the scar won't be noticeable – it really has faded a lot."

"Do you think so? To me, it still looks so very obvious."

"As there is nothing more you can do about it, you must simply not think about it – just focus on being charming, and hope that in an intimate environment like this, you can make a connection with a suitable gentleman."

Venetia sighed.

"I suppose you are right. We had best go down and discover who else is here. I do hope that there isn't anyone I dislike – a week cooped up with someone unpleasant would not be conducive to Christmas cheer."

"I do agree – but the only way we can discover who is here, is to go down now."

Venetia nodded, and, with one last look in the mirror, turned to the door.

In the corridor, a footman waited to show them to the large parlour, and they followed him through the house. The walls were filled with paintings – some portraits, obviously of previous Earls, some landscapes, and some of the older style hunting pictures. Everything about the building spoke of wealth and elegance.

When they reached the parlour, the footman opened the door, and announced them, then, as they stepped inside, shut the door behind them. Venetia looked around, seeing, with relief, a few of the young ladies she had known in London – the wallflowers, not the beauties – and a few men she remembered, even if she had not ever conversed with them. Then, as people on the other side of the room shifted, she saw something – or rather, someone – that she did not expect.

She half-stumbled, and clutched her mother's arm momentarily.

"Venetia? What is it?"

"Mother – over there... it's Jasper, I'm sure of it!"

Chapter Thirteen

Morgan was beginning to feel as if this whole house party might actually be a success. So far, everyone was happily sipping their pre-dinner drinks and talking, as he circulated about the room, making sure that all was well. His mother smiled at him from across the room where she was speaking to the mother of one of the young ladies.

He turned, scanning the room, wondering who to speak to next, when there was movement at the door, and the footman announced Lady Hardenwell and Lady Venetia. For a moment, he was struck to stillness by Lady Venetia's beauty – the gown she wore was simple and elegant, in a green which matched the colour of her eyes – a daring colour for a young woman, for it was quite a strong green, far from the pastels which most young ladies wore. Her scar had faded, he could see, and he, at least, found it barely noticeable. To his eyes, it did not detract, in any way, from her beauty.

He hurried across the room to greet them, already smiling. As he approached, Lady Venetia seemed to almost stumble, a most strange expression flitting across her face for a moment. It was so fleeting that he wondered if he had imagined it. Then, she touched her mother's arm, and said something to her softly, before they continued into the room.

"Welcome, Lady Hardenwell, Lady Venetia!"

They stopped, their eyes drawn to him when he spoke, and both smiled. He bowed, and they curtsied in return. His eyes went to Lady Venetia's, and for a moment, he saw nothing but those green eyes. He was brought back to himself by Lady Hardenwell's voice.

"We are most refreshed, Lord Templewick – our thanks for the excellent accommodations."

"I am glad that you are pleased. I think that you are already acquainted with many of the guests, but let me introduce you to those you do not know."

Lady Hardenwell glanced at Lady Venetia for a moment, and it was as if some unspoken message passed between them. Lady Venetia drew herself up, and looked back to him.

"Thank you, I would appreciate introductions."

He led them across the room, towards where the group of gentlemen stood, assuming that, whilst they would have come to know the ladies whilst in London, they may not have been introduced to all of the gentlemen. They halted beside the group, and the men paused their conversation politely, turning to Morgan.

"Ladies, may I make known to you, Viscount Wilborough, Lord Charles Oldham, Lord James Quincy, Albert Manning, the Earl of Durringham and Lord Jasper Chater. Gentlemen, this is Lady Hardenwell, and her daughter, Lady Venetia Chater."

He realised as he said the words, that Lord Jasper's surname was the same as Lady Venetia's, and curiosity filled him – were they related in some way?

The men bowed, the ladies curtsied, and there was a general expression of pleasure in the introduction – until it came to Lord Jasper. His bow was rather perfunctory, and his smile was little better than a sneer.

"My aunt, and my sadly blemished cousin, are well known to me already, Templewick. I must say, I didn't expect to see you at an event like this, dear cousin."

Morgan found himself with a sudden desire to plant Lord Jasper a facer. His disparaging tone and arrogant, disrespectful expression indicated that he was not the sort of man Morgan would normally have wanted in his company. And to see that attitude turned on Lady Venetia made his blood boil. But before Morgan could say anything, Lady Hardenwell drew herself up, lifted her chin, and spoke.

"I could say the same of you, Lord Jasper – I certainly didn't expect to find you here, at a respectable Christmas house party. I would have thought you more likely to seek out the sort of country event designed for licentiousness, than one intended for pleasant polite company. Perhaps you still have the capacity to surprise me, but I doubt it. Your manners certainly have not improved, nor has your attitude to your cousin. I will thank you, while we are here, to keep a civil tongue in your head."

There was, rather obviously, a history of unpleasant interactions here, and Morgan would be having serious words with Wilborough later, about having brought what looked to be a problem into his house. He hadn't liked Lord Jasper on sight, and now, he had been shown that the man's character was lacking.

Lord Jasper bristled, then waved a hand, as if shaking off something unpleasant.

"I am sure that we can manage to avoid each other, as we obviously wish to, even at such an intimate gathering as this – after all, I do not expect that you will be interested in the same type of diversions as I will."

Beside Lord Jasper, Lord Wilborough was looking rather uncomfortable, and Morgan suspected that the man was regretting bringing Lord Jasper with him.

"Now, now, Chater, let's not start out with unpleasantness – I would have thought you'd be glad to see your relatives."

"Wilborough, you should know that not everyone likes, or gets on with, their entire family... I like some far more than others..."

It was said with a grin, and Morgan had the feeling that there was some kind of double meaning in the words.

Beside him, Lady Venetia was almost quivering, and Morgan had the strangest feeling that she was torn between anger and fear – but why would she fear her cousin? He glanced at her, and she gave him a tremulous smile. He would definitely need to seek out a chance to speak to her in relative privacy, and discover just what this was all about.

Lady Hardenwell fixed Lord Jasper with a hard glare for a few moments, then gave the tiniest shrug. She turned to the other gentlemen.

"I am pleased to meet you, gentlemen – perhaps we will all enjoy being in company better, for not being related."

The men laughed, softly, and the tension eased.

Morgan led the ladies away, to introduce them to some others in the room. As he did, he brushed his hand against Lady Venetia's arm, wanting to assure himself that all was well with her, now that they had removed themselves from her cousin's proximity. It was as if heat spread from the point of that touch, warmth filling him. She looked up at him quickly, and there was shock in her expression – had she felt that warmth too?

He smiled, and removed his hand, but spoke in a whisper.

"Are you well? That was not well done of Lord Jasper."

She walked on beside him, and responded, in a whisper even softer than his had been.

"Nothing Lord Jasper does could be regarded as well done, unless you regard a talent for losing money when gambling as a skill."

Morgan took a deeper breath, swallowing his shock at her words. He was beginning to think that Lord Jasper would be better off anywhere but here. Managing his behaviour for the next week might be more of a challenge than Morgan had expected.

They reached another group of people, and Morgan performed introductions to those Lady Hardenwell did not know, then left them there, and went to greet another new arrival. But all the while, his mind was on Lady Venetia, and that moment when she had seemed almost afraid.

*****

When she had seen Jasper, standing there, looking as arrogant as usual, Venetia had wanted nothing more than to run from the room and hide. This couldn't be happening, just couldn't! This house party was her chance, and now, with Jasper here, not only would she have to be careful to avoid being trapped by him at all times, but he would most likely poison the attitudes of all of the other men against her.

But, just as she had been about to pull her mother away, and escape the room, Lord Templewick had come to greet them, and she had been left with no choice but to stay, to smile, and to behave as if finding her cousin here was not disturbing. Her brave face had, of course, been pointless, for Jasper had immediately embarrassed her, and her mother, in front of everyone.

And then her mother had shocked Venetia completely her words had been barely polite, and very pointed, but far more proper than Lord Jasper's, and everyone around them had seemed to be more sympathetic to them, than to Jasper. That might have made her feel a little better, had Jasper then not made that remark about liking some of his relatives more than others – all the while leering at her in a rather improper manner.

That remark had brought a sharp flood of memories to her mind, of Jasper trapping her, of his body against hers, and his expectation that she would simply accept his advances. Those memories came with fear – and overwhelming anger. She had thought that fear behind her when they had left London, but now, to find it here! She had felt herself shaking, and it was only the gentle touch of Lord Templewick's hand which had drawn her back to full awareness of where she was.

She met his eyes, and what she saw there filled her with warmth, with hope – even with Jasper here, perhaps this house party might not be a complete disaster after all.

*****

The morning dawned cold and clear, with a light frost on the ground. Venetia sat at the window of her room, sipping the hot chocolate the kitchen had sent up, and staring out across the gardens to the fields beyond. The desire to ride across those fields was strong, and she wished that she had been able to bring her favourite horse with her.

It was a desire made stronger by the surprisingly good conversations of the previous evening. At dinner, she had been seated beside Lady Merringbar – she who had been Miss Amelia Hanson, when they had met in London only three months before. They had spoken more during that dinner than Venetia thought they had for the entire time she had been in London.

It turned out that Amelia, as she insisted Venetia address her, was also a keen and competent rider, and was most happy to have retired to their country estate with her new husband. It was good to know that there was someone at this house party with whom she had interests in common, although nothing could remove the shiver of fear that ran through her, whenever she thought about the fact that Jasper was here.

What would she do if he tried to trap her alone? She would fight him, of course, but he was stronger than she was, and, now that he knew from past experience that she would fight – and aim for his most vulnerable parts – he would no doubt be more clever about it. She would just have to make sure that she was never alone – there was nothing else she could think of, which might help.

Sighing, her pleasure in the morning spoilt by the thought of Jasper, she set the cup back on the tray, and stood, calling for Molly to help her dress. It was time to go down and break her fast, and discover what entertainments had been arranged for the day.

Breakfast, she discovered, when she went down with Lady Hardenwell beside her, was in a lovely light filled room with windows overlooking the gardens at the rear of the house. A sumptuous repast was laid out on a sideboard, and two footmen hovered, ready to assist. Soon, with a loaded plate, she settled at the table beside Amelia, who appeared to have an appetite to match her own.

"Good morning! Did you sleep well, Venetia?"

"I did – the bed was most comfortable."

"Mine was too. I think I'm going to enjoy this party – it's interesting that most of the people here are the wallflowers and the quieter girls, with none of the acknowledged beauties – it makes me feel so much more comfortable when I am not continually attempting to look as beautiful as they do."

"It is interesting – but you have no need to try to look any way different from how you are – you are beautiful, Amelia, and obviously Lord Merringbar was clever enough to see that."

Amelia blushed.

"Thank you for saying so." Amelia paused, as if considering her next words carefully. "And... you are beautiful too, Venetia. The scar doesn't change your face, and now that it's fading, I hope that people will stop being so silly about it."

Venetia felt a sudden urge to tears, which she sternly repressed.

"That's very kind of you, Amelia. Dealing with people's attitude to it has been very challenging, and I appreciate your courtesy."

Amelia looked a little abashed.

"Thank you! I know that when I first met you, I wasn't... very nice... - until I saw what sort of person you were, and stopped worrying about the scar. I'm sorry for that, if you can forgive me?"

"Of course I can – I would be honoured to have you as a friend, if you would permit it?"

"That would be wonderful! You should come to visit us, and we can ride about our estate together. It's a pity that we don't have our horses here – I wonder if Lord Templewick has some horses we could borrow?"

Venetia had not considered that possibility, and now that it had been mentioned, the idea appealed to her a great deal.

"We should ask him. He is kind, and I am sure that he would be happy to help, if he has suitable horses."

Amelia nodded, and they resolved to do so, as soon after breakfast as a chance presented itself. They turned their attention, then, to the excellent food before them, and said very little for some time.

But, Venetia noted with a shiver of unease, Jasper was watching her, from where he sat on the other end of the long table. She could almost feel his eyes upon her, like cold fingers on her skin, and even the warmth of Amelia's kind remarks could not remove that chill.

*****

Morgan watched the guests with interest, seeing a very different side to the social interaction here, compared to in London ballrooms and drawing rooms. He rather thought that the way that people behaved here was more natural, and showed more of each person's true character. Which, for most of them, meant that he liked them better here. Of course, there were exceptions – starting with Lord Jasper, who did not improve with further acquaintance.

The man was crass in his manner, and had already, before the afternoon had barely begun, suggested that playing cards for 'decent stakes' might liven up the day. Morgan had simply said that gambling was not on the list of entertainments planned for the week, and left it at that, but Lord Jasper had looked both horrified and angered by his statement. Perhaps the man had hoped to go home substantially richer – a hope which would not be fulfilled.

The last of the guests had arrived this morning, and once they were settled in, Morgan had decided that, as the weather was fine, with a little warmth from the weak winter sun, he would begin the activities by leading a walk through the gardens and the surrounds of the house, so that everyone would know where to find things.

Now, as they gathered in the large parlour, he took note of who was there, and smiled when he saw Lady Venetia. Perhaps he might use this as a chance to walk near her, and to speak a little?

He strode over to where she stood with her mother, in conversation with Lady Merringbar.

"Good day, Ladies, I hope that you will be joining me on our walk about the grounds?"

It was Lady Venetia who turned to him first, with a smile on her face – a smile which made her look quite stunningly lovely.

"We will, my Lord. I look forward to seeing the gardens, but also the stables and the fields – mother has always chastised me for being more interested in horses than in the more genteel activities usually expected of ladies."

Lady Merringbar laughed.

"In that, we are very alike. I trust that you keep a good stable, my Lord?"

For a moment, Morgan hesitated – he did not wish to reveal too much of his past as a stablemaster, yet he also felt called to share his love for horses with these young women who seemed of like mind on the matter. He swallowed – what harm could there be in admitting to an interest?

"I like to think that I do. I have always been happiest around horses – from long before I came into the title."

Lady Venetia regarded him sharply for a moment – perhaps remembering one of their earlier conversations, about him not being like most men of the *ton*? But it was Lady Merringbar who spoke.

"I am glad to hear it, my Lord – too many gentlemen see horses only as a conveyance, or as a financial asset, rather than as creatures with character all their own."

"I would certainly agree with you there, my Lady." He glanced around the room, quickly calculating the number of people present. "I think that everyone is here, so perhaps we should begin."

"Of course."

He turned to face the room, and clapped his hands together.

"Ladies and gentlemen, I believe that we are ready to begin our tour of the grounds – if you would all follow me."

And with that, he turned back to Lady Venetia, and offered her his arm. She blushed, but placed her hand upon it, and they stepped out through the glass doors onto the small terrace, then proceeded down the stairs into the gardens.

He was acutely conscious of the warmth of her hand on his arm, and a sense of deep pleasure filled him at being in her company.

*****

Venetia was charmed by Lord Templewick's manner, and when he offered her his arm, she felt the eyes of every other young Lady present focus on her, filled with envy. It was more than she could have hoped for – but did it mean that he cared for her? Or was he simply being kind again?

As they moved to the door, she glanced across the room, and there, she discovered Jasper – watching her, his expression tight and disapproving. It sent a shiver through her, especially when he bent to the gentleman beside him, and whispered something, with an angling of his head in her direction. The other man gave a soft laugh, and turned to study Venetia, blatantly, his eyes coldly assessing her. Fear coiled in her stomach, and she forced her gaze back to where they were going, determined to concentrate on Lord Templewick, and what he was showing them.

She would not let Jasper spoil everything!

Chapter Fourteen

They crossed the lawns, and Lord Templewick led them through the gardens, which would be magnificent come spring, and which featured fountains and follies, as well as a lake. There was also, around the side of the house, a kitchen garden, inside its own walled enclosure. He pointed out the greenhouses, set to the other side of the house, and the paths which led down past the lake to the pastures beyond.

"If you look into the distance, where the two hills drop into a deep valley between them, with rock outcrops on each hill, you are seeing the boundary of the estate. It expands about an equal distance to that to each side, as well."

The size of it was breathtaking – so much bigger than Brightwood Chase or even Hard Abbey! Venetia imagined what it would be like to ride out on an estate this size – one could go for hours, and still be on the Templewick property. Which would make it far easier to get on with one's neighbours, she suspected. As if reading her thoughts, Amelia spoke from beside her.

"To have one's house so far from one's neighbours would make keeping a good relationship with them less challenging."

Lord Templewick laughed.

"In that, you are correct. My estate manager tells me that there have been no disputes for many years, and I hope to keep it that way."

Lady Hardenwell sighed.

"I wish that I could say the same about Brightwood Chase. When I inherited it, I also inherited a fifty-year long feud about one tiny pasture, on the banks of a stream. It's been more than a year since, and I think that we have finally made progress – although the answer may be simply to give in and sign over that one acre to the neighbour – I really don't see the point in arguing forever."

Lord Templewick nodded.

"I agree. Best to simply create a solution, and move on. As we are about to do – the stables are next, and then the home farm."

He led them back through the gardens, and past a long hedge, behind which the stable buildings surrounded three sides of a square, with a grassed area in the middle. One side was the carriage house, and the other two were stabling at ground level, and feed storage, plus grooms accommodation on the upper level.

As they stepped into the central building, Venetia breathed deeply of the familiar scent of horses and hay, and then sighed with pleasure. Lord Templewick glanced at her, and a small, almost secret smile slipped across his face.

"This is beautiful! So much space, and so well designed. And so many horses – are there others out to pasture still, or is it cold enough that you've brought them all in by now?"

"They are in – apart from a few of the ponies and the draft horses, who have such shaggy coats that the weather doesn't bother them. But all of the brood mares, carriage horses and riding horses are in these two buildings. So, with all of the guests horses, things are a little crowded at present – so much so that I've moved some of the mares to one of the buildings at the home farm, temporarily."

They walked along the row of stalls, and, towards the end, Venetia stopped to stroke the nose of a horse.

It was looking out at them curiously, and sniffed her fingers, as if hoping for food. She laughed, rubbing its face above the eye, so that it turned its head and pushed into her touch.

"I have nothing for you – and you have a full haynet – you are obviously an opportunist."

The gelding snorted softly, and shook its head. Lord Templewick stepped up beside her, so close that she could feel the heat of his body, and her mouth was suddenly dry. Behind them, other guests had scattered somewhat, talking to various of the horses, or wandering back out into the square.

"This is Chamberlain – and you are quite right that he is an opportunist, not just about food, but also about getting his own way when ridden."

"He sounds like just my kind of horse – a little bit of a challenge, but full of character."

There was a moment of silence, and the horse stretched out his nose and nudged her, looking for more attention. Then, Lord Templewick spoke again, quietly, so that only she, and those very close to them, could hear.

"Then perhaps you would like to ride him? We could get together a small party to ride out across the estate in the morning?"

Venetia almost gasped, delighted, but then stopped.

"I would love to – but I did not bring a riding habit with me."

Close by, Amelia spoke up.

"Ah, but I did – two, in fact, and I think that we are close enough in size that you could borrow one of mine. Of course, if Lord Templewick has another suitable horse available, I would love to ride out as well."

"I do indeed have a number of other suitable horses. I shall arrange for the horses to be ready in the morning, and a groom to ride out with us." His voice dropped even lower, to a level meant only for Venetia's ears. "I look forward to that more intimate time in your company."

Heat flushed through Venetia, and she quickly looked up, meeting his eyes - they were filled with an appreciative warmth which took her breath away. They stayed there, still, and the silence stretched, until she forced some words out, even as she looked back at the horse.

"I look forward to that too."

It was a daring thing to say, yet she felt confident in saying it to this man, for he, of all people, was someone she could trust not to misinterpret her meaning.

"Then let us move on – we will go down to the home farm now, and after that, return to the house for some refreshments."

Lord Templewick had raised his voice so that the others could hear, and she turned, ready to follow him again as he stepped away to speak to another guest, only to discover that Jasper stood only a few feet away. How much had he heard of their conversation? It worried her that he might have heard it all, and might have, in a manner typical of him, misinterpreted every word. His eyes were on her, and they were cold, uncaring for anything except his own pleasures – pleasures which she knew he would take from her, if he had the chance.

Then that considering expression disappeared, and Jasper presented her with a leering grin, sketched a mocking little bow, and bent towards her for a moment.

"I would certainly enjoy more intimate time in your company, if you are granting such favours – and perhaps even if there is no granting about it. We really must arrange something."

With that, which had shocked her to breathlessness, he turned and walked away. Her heart was pounding, and she hurried to catch up to Lord Templewick, in whose company at least she felt safe.

The rest of the walk was uneventful, and she stayed close to Lord Templewick, and her mother, but those moments with Jasper stayed in her thoughts, and overlayed all her pleasure in the day with a chill of fear, and a premonition of bad things to come.

A premonition she very much hoped would not prove true.

*****

The following morning was clear, and the air crisp without being icy. Venetia breathed deeply as she walked across from the house to the stables, with Amelia by her side. The habit which Amelia had lent her was a beautiful dark green, and fitted her almost perfectly, which filled her with delight, for it meant that she could ride.

In the stables Lord Templewick awaited them, with his own horse, Chamberlain for Venetia, and a lovely grey mare for Amelia. A groom was waiting, already mounted, to follow them for propriety's sake. They led the horses out onto the grass of the square, and mounted, Venetia simply stepping up by herself, with the ease of long practice, Amelia using the mounting block.

"Oh! I do wish I could do that! I just don't have enough spring to mount by myself."

Venetia laughed.

"I learnt of necessity, after falling off many times in our fields, and facing the choice of managing to mount or walking home on my own feet. It took a lot of practice for me to make it look anything like smooth and elegant."

Lord Templewick mounted his own horse, and rode over to where they waited, a smile on his face.

"Well I, for one, think that you have managed to make it look effortless."

Venetia felt the heat of a blush stain her cheeks, and looked away, unsure how to respond. Her eyes roamed around the stable area, and for a moment she thought that she saw movement in the shadowed doorway, then it was gone. She had probably imagined it. She brought her attention back to what she was doing when Amelia spoke.

"Are we going a specific way, Lord Templewick? Are there particularly scenic parts of the estate?"

He waved a hand towards the lane that led to the home farm.

"We'll go down past the home farm, and then across the valley and up onto the ridge opposite, where there is an excellent view of the whole district. We can come back along the path of the stream, through the centre of the valley, and approach the house from the other side."

And so they went, with the groom trailing some distance behind them – in sight, but out of hearing.

Once they reached the top of the ridge on the other side of the valley, they paused by the ruins of an old stone tower, and dismounted. Lord Templewick pointed out local landmarks, and explained the history of the ruins they stood amongst. After a short while, when he had finished his description, Amelia looked past the ruined wall beside them.

"Is that another wall over there?"

"It is – we think there was an outbuilding there, although its been ruins for many generations. There is a good view into the next valley from behind it, if you are willing to climb through some rocks."

Amelia grinned.

"Of course I'm willing – I love exploring."

And with that, she set off. Lord Templewick turned to Venetia with an enquiring look.

"No thank you – I'm happy right here, with the scenery in front of me."

"Then I shall stay here with you, Lady Venetia. Might I be improper, and ask... has there been some past trouble with Lord Jasper? I did not understand exactly what he was trying to imply, yesterday, but it seemed to me that there was a sharpness to his manner, when he spoke of, or to, you."

Venetia met his eyes, caught, as always, by the kindness and warmth in their deep brown depths, and sighed. What could she tell him? Anything she might say could be misinterpreted – yet... she trusted him, and she needed to say something.

"I... thank you for your concern. The answer to your question is yes – when we were in London, we stayed at Hardenwell House – which, when my father was Marquess, was our home, but which is now my uncle's home, and hence Jasper's. My uncle and aunt were in the country, but Jasper was in London. He was... extremely disparaging of my appearance, since the scar... and made the assumption, as did so many men, that it meant I was utterly ruined, and thereby open to their advances. He was... improperly persistent, and it was only by the application of my knee in unmentionable places that I escaped his grasp. I do not trust him, at all. But there is nothing to be done about him, so long as he is behaving appropriately – you could not send him from your home without good cause, much though I might wish you to."

Lord Templewick frowned, then reached out and took her hand, almost as if unaware of what he was doing. The warmth of his touch thrilled her, and her breath came short.

"I commend your courage in dealing with him. That is something which should never have been necessary. Be assured that I will watch him, and, if he does anything at all which I dislike, I will send him away. I have not been impressed by his manner, so far. I do not, in fact, quite understand why he came here with Wilborough, for this is not the sort of house party which I would have thought him likely to find appealing."

Venetia nodded, acutely aware that his hand still held hers.

"I would not have thought so either. Unless he hoped to find someone to gamble with – he has many debts, we have discovered, and perhaps he hoped to win enough from some unsuspecting person to defray some of those?"

Lord Templewick's expression cleared.

"That sounds likely. And if that is what he hoped, he will be disappointed."

Venetia tightened her fingers on his, and he started slightly, apparently only then realising that he held her hand. But he did not release it, and a small bubble of happiness exploded within her because of that.

"Thank you. Just having someone other than my mother and myself know of Jasper's... attitudes... makes me feel safer."

His hand tightened on hers again for a moment.

"I promise you that I will do my utmost to keep you safe, should Lord Jasper do anything untoward."

Those words carried a freight of meaning, in a way that she did not understand. But she had no opportunity to discover more, for Amelia came scrambling back through the ruins at that moment, and Lord Templewick rapidly dropped her hand, and turned away a little to address Amelia.

"Did you discover the view that you hoped for?"

"I did – it really is lovely, and worth having torn my hem getting to it. My maid will be unhappy, but it's only a little tear."

Venetia laughed, hearing the echo of herself in those words. Lord Templewick smiled too, with gentle amusement.

"We'd best be getting back, ladies, or everyone will be up, and doing who knows what in my house in my absence."

They mounted up, Amelia accepting a boost by stepping into Lord Templewick's cupped hands, and set off along the ridge, to where a trail followed a stream down from the spring that gave birth to its waters.

"This is beautiful! You are lucky to have such a wonderful estate."

Venetia spoke impulsively, captured by the beauty around her. He turned in the saddle a little, and met her eyes.

"I am indeed lucky to have it, for I was never in the direct line of succession."

"Often, the most unexpected things happen, to change one's life."

She said it, thinking of her fall, and the scar. He shrugged.

"All I can do is accept what is, and manage it as best I can."

"Indeed, that is all anyone can do."

*****

Morgan had been thoroughly enjoying the ride, and watching just how well Lady Venetia rode, until that moment up at the ruins, when she had told him of Lord Jasper's past perfidy. Anger had boiled through him, for a moment near blinding him to where he was. That her own cousin could have treated her so! And that she spoke of it so calmly, with such resignation, spoke to just how strong she was, but also to how sadly resigned she had become to being treated badly.

He resolved in that moment to send a message to his man of business, as soon as they were back in the house – a message requesting that he investigate, and take certain actions with respect to Lord Jasper's debts. A man like that should not be permitted to continue in his wastrel and rakish ways.

He ached for Lady Venetia - to suffer such treatment, all because of an accident - and, a trickle of guilt slid through him, because his repair of her face had not, in the end, been good enough.

He had thought upon the matter of Lord Jasper, even as he watched Lady Venetia riding ahead of him, all the way back down through the valley. He was barely aware of the beauty around him, unless one of the women drew his attention to something, but by the time they rode into the stables, he was no further forward with respect to what he might do to help – for Lady Venetia had been right in what she'd said – he could not summarily eject Lord Jasper from his house without good reason.

Which simply meant that he needed to watch the man like a hawk, and find a reason to remove him as soon as possible.

They dismounted and, having handed his own horse off to a groom, he walked with Lady Venetia and Lady Merringbar through the stables. When they reached Chamberlain's stall, Lady Venetia stopped, leading the horse in.

"I will leave you here with him, whilst I show Lady Merringbar where Cloud's stall is. A groom will be along shortly to assist, and care for him."

She smiled at him, and his heart caught in his chest, missing a beat, for her face was stunning, when lit with that beautiful smile.

"I will remove the saddle, and rub him down with a hay wisp, so that he knows I appreciate riding him. Don't concern yourself – I will see you back at the house."

"If you are certain..."

It worried him a little, to leave her so, yet there were many grooms moving about the stables complex, so all should be well.

"I am quite certain."

He bowed then, and led Lady Merringbar and her horse further along. As he turned away, Lady Venetia was already twisting a wisp out of some hay taken from Chamberlain's haynet.

*****

Venetia twisted the wisp, even as Chamberlain tried to eat it from her hands, then took the halter and lead rope which was hanging on the corner of the stall door, and quickly slipped Chamberlain's bridle off, and the halter on, then tied him where he could eat from his haynet. Moments later, she had undone and lifted off the sidesaddle, and deposited it over the top of the stall door, which she pulled not quite closed, so that it did not obstruct the walkway.

Then she set to, running the wisp vigorously over the horse's back and sides, removing the sweat and saddle marks. The gelding shut his eyes, and leaned into the pressure of it a little, like a cat leans into a hand scratching it under the chin. She laughed softly, and relaxed, enjoying the scent of horse and hay, and the simple task of giving an animal pleasure in return for its service to her.

She lost herself in the moment, so much so that, when, bare minutes later, a hand slipped around her waist and she was pulled back against a lean body, she dropped the wisp and nearly screamed – nearly, because a hand came up to cover her mouth, and cut the sound off.

Chapter Fifteen

Morgan stayed with Lady Merringbar for the short while she spent stroking the neck of the mare, then, once a groom came to deal with the horse, led her out at the other end of the building, and across the square back towards the house. When they rounded the hedge, and she could see the house before her, he begged her pardon, and left her to walk the last part herself. He did not know why, but he felt uncomfortable leaving Lady Venetia in the stables, and instinct told him to go back.

He turned, and hurried across the gravelled area, and back to the main stables entry, his feet crunching on the pebbles as he went, the sound distinct in the crisp morning air. Would she think him foolish for this? Probably, for she was of an independent nature, especially when it came to horses, yet he could not risk any harm coming to her.

And as he thought that, he realised just how much he cared for her. Seeing her again, with the break in time since they had been in London, had made it very obvious to him. With a wry twist of his lips, he acknowledged that thought, and the problem which came with it – how might he tell her that he cared? And what if she did not care for him in return?

He would deal with that challenge when he came to it. He tapped the stables door as he went through into the dimness of the space, momentarily half blind after the brighter light outside.

At the end of the long row with stalls either side, he thought he saw a movement – but with the half blindness of having just stepped inside, her could not be sure – it was probably one of the grooms going about their work.

Whistling softly to himself, he continued down towards Chamberlain's stall.

*****

There was movement beside her too, and as she swallowed her scream, frozen for a moment from the shock of things, a voice came very softly from that direction.

"I say, old boy, I thought you said she was a willing piece – what's this then?"

The hand around her waist tightened, squeezing her so hard that she couldn't breathe for long moments, then a voice came beside her ear. A voice she knew.

"Oh, she puts on a great show of it, but it's just show – with that scar she's thoroughly ruined, and she'll take what she's offered, because she has no other options."

With that, he spun her around, and removed his hand from her mouth, only to replace it with his lips. She nearly gagged, for he tasted of brandy, even this early in the day. It was Jasper, of course – she should have known that he would not leave her alone – and this time, he had brought company.

There was no possible way that she could fight off two of them at once. Still she squirmed in Jasper's grasp. The other man spoke again, even softer, his voice full of doubt.

"That doesn't exactly look willing to me..."

At that moment, there was a sound – the crunching of feet on gravel.

Venetia stilled, even as Jasper's mouth left hers – should she scream? But if she did, and was found like this… she might as easily be forced to marry Jasper, as be saved from him. She waited to see what he would do. The footsteps got closer.

The other man reached out and shook Jasper's shoulder.

"Someone's coming. I'm away, I'll have no part of this."

He slipped out of the stall, and Jasper met her eyes, then swore under his breath.

"You damned slattern, I'll have you yet. But this, just now – this never happened. Tell no one, or I will make sure that your reputation is as ruined as your face, be assured of it."

Then he was gone, slipping out of the stall, and hurrying along to the other end of the building on near silent feet.

Venetia took a staggering step, and wrapped her arms around Chamberlain's neck, allowing the horse to support her for the few moments until the shaking eased, and her knees felt capable of holding her again. The gelding turned his head, whuffled at her fingers, then went back to eating.

The footsteps which had put Jasper and his friend to flight had taken the last few steps on gravel, and then continued on the brick of the stable corridor. Now, they stopped just outside Chamberlain's stall. Venetia drew in a very deep breath, and released the horse, hoping that it did not look as if she had been depending on him to stay upright, then turned, just as the stall door opened.

Lord Templewick stood there. Oh Lord! What did she look like? Was her hair in disarray? Her hat was most certainly askew. He met her eyes, his face concerned, and she had the dreadful feeling that he knew that something was wrong.

"Lady Venetia? Is all well? I came to check, as it had been some time."

She swallowed. She could not tell him what had happened – Jasper's threat still echoed in her mind – she could not risk utter ruin.

“All is well, although Chamberlain has no respect for a ladies hat, or her hair – he found it necessary to ascertain whether they were edible, and took some persuading of the fact that hay was a better feed for a horse. But thank you for your concern.”

At that moment, a groom hurried up to them.

“I’m sorry, my Lord, my Lady, I would have been here sooner, but that new stallion is a little fractious.” He took in the rubbed down horse, and the saddle and bridle neatly set on the stable door, and bowed. “There was no need to be doing my job for me, but I’m grateful.”

Venetia managed to laugh, although to her own ears it sounded a little shaky.

“I’ve saddled and unsaddled my own horses many a time. It’s not a concern. But I’ll leave him to your care now, with thanks.”

Lord Templewick offered her his arm as she stepped out into the corridor, and she placed her hand on it, feeling somehow safer for his touch. He spoke softly as they walked towards the door.

“Is all truly well? You seem a little... disconcerted?”

She did not want to lie to this man, but she had to.

“I am well. But... can you please adjust my hat, and my hair, so that I look respectable? Without a mirror, I really can’t achieve that.”

He gave her a conspiratorial smile.

“I do not profess to be an expert at dressing a lady’s hair, but I will do my best.”

So she paused, and he reached up, tugging her hat gently back into position, resetting the pins in her hair, and the hat pin which held the hat in place. It was a shockingly intimate thing for a gentleman to be doing to her, and it made her breath come short, her mouth go dry, and her heart ache, for the intimacies she might never know with a man who cared for her.

He set the last pin, and stepped back to assess the result.

There was something in his eyes, some warmth, and yet something of sadness, which confused her. Then he nodded.

"Will I do? Do I look respectable enough to walk through the house?"

"You do indeed look respectable – and beautiful, as you always do."

The words shocked her utterly, but he simply offered his arm again, and they set off back to the house, both in a contemplative silence.

*****

Morgan didn't believe her.

He'd spoken with her enough, in London, and here, to know that there was something wrong. Just what might have happened in the stables in that short time he had left her alone, he did not know, but something had, of that he was certain.

But he could not demand answers – he had no right to demand anything of her, no reason to expect anything.

Which did not mean that he did not ache to know, ache to make whatever was wrong, right.

He feared for her, even though he did not know what there was to fear.

It was nearly Christmas, and this should be a joyous time of year, yet here he was, considering a Lady being fearful – it was not right.

And the strength of his fears, the ache that her discomfiture roused in his heart, startled him, and made him, yet again, realise just how much he had come to care for this woman.

Still, he allowed the silence, and simply escorted her back to the house – there would, hopefully, be time later to discover what was wrong. And in the interim, he would watch closely, and perhaps find, in what he saw, an indication of what the problem truly was.

*****

Venetia was surprised that she had managed to walk back to the house at all, for inside, she was still shaking. But manage she did, with the comforting support of Lord Templewick's arm beneath her hand. The fragile composure she had managed to gain he had near destroyed by calling her beautiful, but she had, somehow, stayed steady, and kept walking.

Now, in her rooms, and putting her hair to rights properly, as she changed into a suitable day dress, her mind was in turmoil. It would, she knew, be entirely possible for Jasper to make good on his threat to utterly ruin her reputation – it did not take all that much gossip to stain a woman's reputation, whether there was any truth in it or not. And she did not know what to do, for almost any action she might take could be enough to make him, simply out of petty spite, set out to ruin her, by gossip, if not in physical fact.

She was also greatly disturbed that there had been another gentleman with him in the stables – for that meant another man she needed to avoid – which was somewhat challenging, when she did not even know the man's name, and had not seen his face! The only thing she could do was go on as if it had not happened, as if Jasper was not here, spoiling what had seemed a pleasant way to approach Christmas, spoiling what had seemed a last chance to find a match.

And as she thought that, the only face which rose in her mind was that of Lord Templewick. If she had to marry someone, why, oh why, could it not be him? She pushed that wish aside – deluding herself by dreaming of the man she might never have, no matter how much she was coming to care for him, was ensuring that she would be miserable in the future. For, in but a few days' time, after this house party, she would have to face the reality of her situation, and likely marry Lord Peterley.

That thought caused a small shudder to run through her, but she internally castigated herself sternly, pushed the last pin into her hair, and went out into their small sitting room, where her mother was waiting for her.

"You look very nice, Venetia – your cheeks have a nice flush to them. It seems a ride in the crisp morning air was good for you."

Venetia struggled to repress the hysterical edge of laughter – that flush on her cheeks was from everything but the crisp morning air!

"It was a lovely ride, Mother. Lord Templewick has a beautiful estate – so large! And Lady Merringbar was excellent company. I do hope that we can ride out again before the end of the week."

"So do I – if only because it will give you more chances to capture Lord Templewick's attentions..."

Venetia blushed then, unused to her mother being so blatant in her encouragement of Venetia's interest in a specific gentleman – but she supposed they were at a point now where they were desperate, and her mother's fears for their future were showing.

"Indeed, although I suspect that our hopes are in vain there."

"Perhaps, perhaps not – let us go down to the parlour, and see what is planned for the day."

Venetia nodded, and they left the room, and turned towards the stairs. A flicker of movement caught Venetia's eye, in the corridor in the opposite direction from the stairs, and she half-turned, trying to see what it was. Just the other side of a fairly large statue, which was placed on a hall table, she was sure that someone stood – someone of similar build to Jasper. But the hall was shadowy, and she could not be sure. She shook her head, turned back, and followed her mother – if she let every shadow frighten her, she would be perpetually distraught – all for no reason.

But still, the question remained in her mind – *what if it had been Jasper, watching her?*

For the rest of the day, that unsettled feeling of being watched persisted, and she found herself looking at everyone with suspicion, avoiding shadowy corners, and listening carefully to the voices of all of the gentlemen, attempting to match someone to the voice of the other man who had been with Jasper in the stables. It was exhausting, and fruitless.

By the end of the day, she felt ragged, and very out of sorts. The only bright spot in the evening was that she was seated next to Lord Templewick at dinner, and they had a delightful conversation about horses – he was extraordinarily knowledgeable. And that brought her mind back to the thought of him being the man who had sewn up her scar – the more she knew him, the more certain she became – but how could she ask?

In bed that night, she held the thought of him close as she drifted to sleep, and then dreamed of him – or was it the man sewing her face?

*****

As soon as they had returned to the house after their ride, Morgan had stepped into his study, and written a quick letter to his man of business, requesting that he ask of his contacts for anything pertaining to Lord Jasper Chater, and any debts he might owe. He had not expected an answer for some time, so he was most surprised when, only two days later, a response came in the mail. It helped that his man of business was in the next town, rather than in London, but still, he had expected messages to go to London and back.

The last two days had been difficult – he had needed to play the role of convivial host, keeping people entertained, even while he was watching Lord Jasper and his friends, and ensuring that they had no chance to be near Lady Venetia, unless she was surrounded by company. He had spent as much time as he could near her himself, but he had not yet said anything to her of his growing feelings, indeed, he was not sure how to broach the matter, and felt somewhat ashamed of his hesitance, both now and in London.

Even this morning, when he had thought that they might ride out again, it had dawned grey and miserable, with a steady light rain, and he had found himself trapped in the house, arranging card tables and other indoor activities, with no chance to be close to Lady Venetia with any sort of even partial privacy.

But now, when the letter was handed to him, hope filled him – hope for something which might allow him to act, and to give Lady Venetia good news – assuming that he could ever find a way to speak to her in private. He excused himself from the parlour and went to his study, closing the door after himself and taking a seat at his desk before breaking the seal on the letter.

He read it carefully, a smile growing on his face as he did, then read it again to be certain that he had grasped all of the detail. It was, as he had suspected, well within his capacity to take the action necessary to guarantee that Lord Jasper would no longer be in a position to disparage Lady Venetia, or otherwise distress her. His man of business had been most efficient, and discovered all that was required.

Pleased, he brought out a sheet of paper, uncapped the inkpot, and lifted his pen. Five minutes later, his instructions were listed, and the missive was sanded, folded, and sealed. On his way back out to the parlour, he found a footman, and sent him off to hand deliver the letter to the man of business, with all speed.

After that, the rest of the day was relatively quiet, with most guests choosing either to play cards, to talk amongst themselves, or to read. Morgan found himself, not long before dinner, walking through the house, casually joining various conversations for a short while, making sure that his guests were happy. His mother had been doing the same every day, and had this morning told him, in no uncertain terms, that he needed to spend more time talking to people. He rather thought it excessive, but if she regarded it as necessary, then he would do it.

He was, he realised, looking for Lady Venetia – she being the only person there whom he truly wanted to talk to. He found her in the parlour, sitting quietly near the window all by herself, watching everyone else. That brought a smile to his face, for she had so often done that in London – he wondered what she thought of these people, here?

He walked across to her, taking note of other conversations and the one card game which was continuing in this room, and took a seat beside her.

“Good Day, Lady Venetia. I trust your day has been pleasant, despite the rain depriving us of our ride.”

She started slightly, and turned to him, her cheeks flushed charmingly.

“Oh! I am sorry, I was thinking. Yes, today has been quite pleasant, although I am tempted to take myself to bed early tonight, and read. I have found that I do not have all that much in common with many of the people here, although most treat me with kindness, unlike many I met in London.”

There was an underlying sadness in her tone, and he ached to change that, to make her happy.

“I would hope so – I tried to invite people who would be pleasant to each other – I had no wish to approach Christmas feeling miserable.”

She met his eyes then, and a wry smile flickered across her face.

“Given everything, I cannot see that my Christmas will be pleasant this year – although this house party has given me an unexpected opportunity for some enjoyment.”

Her eyes held his, and everything else faded away for a moment, as he was drawn into their emerald-green depths. He breathed deeply, capturing the scent of her perfume, a rich tone of rose and vanilla, and felt the urge to tell her how he felt. But not here…

“I am glad that even your cousin’s presence has not prevented your enjoyment.”

Her eyes widened at that, and she glanced down, her fingers twining together in her lap. She did not respond immediately. His heart sank – what had Lord Jasper done? For he was sure, now, that he had done something.

Chapter Sixteen

Two days had passed, since that moment in the parlour where Morgan had been convinced that Lord Jasper had done something dreadful, despite Lady Venetia denying it. There was something in her tone when she did, in her eyes, which told him that what she wanted to say was different, but that something constrained her to lie.

He had watched, but seen nothing untoward, apart, perhaps, from the fact that Lord Jasper appeared prone to watching Lady Venetia, especially when she was not aware of him. That made Morgan feel uncomfortable, but was not, of itself, bad behaviour. He'd had quite a sufficiency of time to observe, for the weather had been unmitigatedly dreary and they had not been out to ride again, or even for a walk about the garden. Which circumstances had prevented him from having any opportunity to speak privately to Lady Venetia.

Everyone was becoming a little irritable now, he thought, from being trapped in the house together.

Morgan was on his way through the foyer, intending to check with the Housekeeper to ensure that all was still well with food and the like, and with the preparations for the grand Christmas dinner which was to be held on the last night of the house party, when a very wet footman came in with the mail he had just collected from the village.

"A letter for you my Lord. The rest are the suppliers bills for the Housekeeper to deal with."

Morgan took the letter from the footman, and quickly glanced at the seal. His man of business – that was a surprise, for he had not expected further information yet. He went to his study, to ensure that he was not interrupted when reading the missive – for what it contained was, to him at least, very important. He broke the seal, and unfolded the papers, studying their contents in detail. It was, he thought, even better than he had hoped for.

His man of business assured him that copies of each document were also held in his office, so that there was a second record of the matters, for safety. Morgan smiled at that, for it showed that his man of business had dealt with those of nefarious mind all too often. He folded the documents again, and tucked them into the hidden inner pocket of his coat – these he wanted on his person at all times, at least for the next few days.

Days in which he suspected he might need to act, to prevent wrongdoing, although he had no proof of that yet.

If he could achieve what he intended, perhaps this Christmas might be far better than expected, and not only for him.

*****

"I do hope that this rain stops! We have so little time left here, only until Christmas Eve morning, before we must leave for Brightwood Chase again, and the rain does so limit your opportunities for such things as walking out with gentlemen. And of course, if the rain continues, then our road home will almost certainly be axle deep in mud. Have any of the gentlemen shown interest in you, Venetia – any at all?"

Venetia sighed, shaking her head.

"None. Unless you count the way that Jasper looks at me."

Lady Hardenwell gave a rather brittle edged laugh.

"No, I most definitely do not count that! I wish so much that he was not here, that you might have had this chance without his interference. Heaven knows what he whispers to the other men."

"I can imagine. I suspect that he will be taking malicious pleasure in poisoning them against me."

Suspect… It was more than that, she knew, after what had happened in the stables… but she wasn't going to tell her mother about that, wasn't going to say anything to anyone, lest it get back to Jasper, and he carry out his threat.

The last few days had been rather agonising, for Venetia had spent every waking moment trying her best to be aware of everyone, and everything, when all she really wanted to do was be aware of Lord Templewick, to have the chance to speak privately with him again, as they had at the ruins up on the hilltop. But that was impossible while it rained, and they were all trapped in the house.

And Jasper was always just there, watching her, his eyes full of a strange kind of greed, which made her skin crawl. She was, in a particular way, exhausted, and not sleeping well as a result.

Her mother shook her head.

"Your father was such a good man – I truly do not understand how his brother, and Jasper, can be such horrible people. But let us not dwell on things we can't change – we should go down to the parlour, perhaps seek out some refreshments, and find someone to talk to."

Venetia rose, and smoothed her skirts.

"If there are no interesting conversations, I think that I will take myself into the library, and find a book to read. I cannot imagine that I am likely to meet Jasper there – he has, from what I know, never been one for reading."

Lady Hardenwell laughed.

"You are correct in that."

They went down, and after partaking of the light refreshments which were laid out on a table at one end of the parlour, sought the company of Lady Merringbar and a number of the other young ladies' mothers. Lady Hardenwell immediately became involved in their conversation, and Venetia turned to Amelia, who looked rather as if she was suffering a bad case of ennui.

"Are you interested in this conversation? Because, forgive me for saying so, you look rather uninspired – which I understand, as I must say that I do not care much at all for the details of embroidery stitches..."

Amelia laughed softly.

"I would far rather be out riding, or be doing anything except embroider, or talk about embroidery."

Venetia nodded.

"I can only agree with you there. I was considering going and hiding in the library – the library here has a rather magnificent collection of books - and it's quiet, with a comfortable couch and chairs. Would you like to accompany me?"

Amelia's eyes lit up at the suggestion and Venetia was glad, for even though she thought it unlikely that Jasper would be found anywhere near a library, she would still feel safer with someone else with her.

"Of course. That's an excellent suggestion."

Venetia whispered in her mother's ear to tell her where she was going, and with whom, then they turned and made their way across the parlour, and out into the corridor. They walked, talking quietly, passing the stairs and continuing along to the other end of the floor, where the library took up the full width of the wing. They did not notice Lord Jasper, who was halfway up the stairs as they passed them - but he noticed them. When he reached the top of the stairs, he paused, and watched them, until they opened the door and disappeared into the library. Only then did he give a nod, and turn towards the parlour.

Venetia closed the library door after them with a sigh of relief, then wandered over to the shelves.

"What shall I read? I wonder if there are any gothic novels here? Or would they be far too improper and scandalous for a man like Templewick to own?"

"Perhaps – but wouldn't most of these books have been purchased by his predecessor? Perhaps generations of previous Earls and their wives – so who knows what we might find."

They set about searching, almost systematically, and soon found a shelf of novels. After much exclaiming about the number of choices, they each selected a book, and went to sit down. Amelia curled in a large wingback armchair, and Venetia seated herself towards one end of a plushly upholstered couch.

"This is so much better that social chit-chat, isn't it, Amelia?"

"Most definitely."

With that, they settled into reading. The room was relatively warm, and the silence pleasant after days in close company with many people. An hour or more passed, the time only marked by the soft ticking of the mantel clock, before Amelia looked up to discover that Venetia had fallen asleep. She had slid sideways until she was nearly lying along the couch, the book fallen from her grasp and resting on the couch cushions close beside her.

Amelia considered what to do – for she needed the necessary, and she wanted to go in search of food. Should she wake Venetia? But surely, if Venetia had fallen asleep, she was genuinely tired. Perhaps it was best to leave her to rest, in this nice quiet spot. She set the book that she was reading down on the side table, and left the room, as quietly as she could, pulling the door closed behind her.

*****

Morgan stepped out of his office, finally done with the organising tasks of the day.

He had just approved the menu for the celebratory Christmas dinner which would be held tomorrow, and finalised the hiring of a small orchestra so that there might be some dancing. And he'd agreed to the rather remarkable cost of swathes of fabric and bundles of greenery for decorating the house. The Housekeeper had gone off happily with everything in hand, and he could finally spend some time on more relaxing activities. Although he wasn't sure that he could consider socialising entirely relaxing....

The important papers which had come from his man of business were tucked safely in against his side, and now it was simply a matter of when and how he might need, or choose, to use the leverage that they gave him. As if that thought had been a summoning, a movement at the end of the corridor caught his eye.

It was, he realised after a moment, Lord Jasper. Which was not, in and of itself, surprising – but what was surprising was that Lord Jasper was entering the library. A man less likely to read for pleasure he had never met. Which suggested to Morgan's somewhat suspicious mind that Lord Jasper was about something other than seeking a book to read.

After a moment of hesitation, Morgan went in that direction, instinct suggesting that he should – and he trusted his instincts, for they had kept him alive many times on the battlefield.

*****

For a moment, Venetia had no concept of where she was. Something was pressing her down, and there was a hard edge digging into her side. She went to move, and discovered that she couldn't, that whatever was pressing her down prevented it. It was at that point that her mind caught up, and her eyes snapped open.

To meet Jasper's face, mere inches away.

Behind him, she could see the library shelves, and memory informed her that she must have fallen asleep while reading.

And, obviously, Amelia had left her there, no doubt thinking it a kindness to let her rest.

With horror, she realised that the weight which was pressing her down onto the couch was Jasper's body. She opened her mouth to scream, but only a half cut off squeal escaped her before his hand clamped over her mouth.

"My dear Venetia – there is no call for screaming. We all know that you're a slattern, and no man is ever going to offer for you. But do squirm and fight me a little if you wish, I find that adds some spice to things. I really don't know why you'd want to scream anyway – if you truly don't find me appealing, then screaming should be your last desire – if someone came in now, and found us like this... well, they'd likely think we should marry, wouldn't they?"

Venetia's blood turned to ice at his words, for he was correct – if she was found like this, she would most likely be forced to marry him. Not that she thought he wanted marriage – but if such a thing happened, and he then refused to marry her, or she refused to marry him, she would be utterly and completely ruined, in all ways.

He must have seen it in her eyes, for he laughed, and moved his body against hers. She stiffened, and considered biting his hand – perhaps she would, if she could see no better way to escape him. But he cautiously moved his hand off her mouth, and that chance was lost.

"Why, Jasper? What do you want of me?"

He lifted a finger and trailed it over her mouth, down her neck and to her breast, which he cupped and squeezed.

She flinched away from his touch, but with his weight on her, there was no escaping.

"What do I want of you? Your body, my dear, at my command, whenever I want it. A woman with no other options is the perfect mistress."

Venetia wished that she had bitten him. Instead, she shifted a little, seeing just how much movement was possible.

He laughed, very sure of himself. His hand went to her breast again, and he shifted his weight to allow himself better access. She took advantage of that, and twisted hard, pulling both knees up, so that they rammed into his private parts as he unbalanced.

"Uncouth lightskirt! How dare you!"

He grabbed at her, trying to keep his balance, to keep her held down.

She obviously hadn't hit him hard enough.

So she screamed – it was worth the risk, and if anyone tried to force her to marry this man, she would refuse. Being a starving, reputationless spinster would be better than marrying this man. He tried to put his hand over her mouth again, but this time, she did bite him, and clamped her teeth shut on the side of his hand. He half-screamed this time.

And it was at that moment that the door opened, so hard and fast that it slammed back against the wall. Terror filled her, of a different kind – who was it? It would make no difference, she realised, so, with a last surge of energy, she lifted a knee again, and made sure that this time it was hard enough, then she spat out his hand.

As she did, hands pulled Jasper off her, and flung him to the floor, where he coiled into a tight ball, clutching his private parts.

Which left her sprawled inelegantly across the couch, her skirts half pulled up and her bodice in disarray, the hard edge of a book still digging into her side. She looked up to see who her rescuer was, and discovered Lord Templewick. Her heart sank – what must he think of her, finding her like this? Surely, if there had ever been any chance of him being interested in her, it was gone now. The only positive of the moment was that there was no one else there – no one had followed him into the room.

She swallowed her pride, and pushed herself up to a sitting position,

"Thank you for your rescue, my Lord."

She met his eyes, and what she saw there startled her.

There was anger, and amusement, and respect, and something else, something warmer. It confused her utterly.

"I think, from what I saw, and heard with my ear pressed to the door, that you were well on your way to rescuing yourself. I commend you. Did he hurt you?"

Venetia shook her head, the shock of the whole situation only now beginning to impact her. She felt suddenly cold, and shaky.

"No. Only my pride, and my side, where I inadvertently lay upon the book." She held it up, lifting it from where it lay beside her. "It was trapped underneath me. I was in here reading with Lady Merringbar, and I must have fallen asleep. I suspect that she left me to rest, out of kindness. And Jasper somehow discovered that I was here alone."

"But you are shaking..."

Lord Templewick settled gently onto the couch beside her, and slipped an arm around her. She leant into him, glad of his support. He pressed a gentle kiss to her brow, right on her scar, and a sob escaped her.

From the floor, Jasper's sneering voice reached her, and she looked to find him pulling himself up to sit, his hands still cupping his injured parts.

"I see, that's the way of it, is it? Well, you're welcome to the slattern, Templewick - after that little performance, I've lost interest. No man will marry her, but she's too much of a fool to accept it – good luck if you think you'll get what you want from her."

Venetia felt Lord Templewick stiffen and his arm dropped away from her. Her heart cried out at its absence, but she supposed that she should have expected it. Then he rose and stepped forward, reaching down to take hold of Jasper's cravat. He twisted it, and with startling ease, hauled Jasper to his feet.

"You, sir, are a bounder, and worse, but I won't use those words in front of a Lady."

Jasper made a half-strangled complaint.

"Release me!"

Lord Templewick laughed.

"Oh I will, in good time. But first, you'll hear what I have to say. Let's start with everything that is wrong with your opinion of Lady Venetia. You say that no man will marry her – there you are incorrect, for I will happily do so, if she will have me." Venetia gasped, sagging back against the couch, unable to take in what he had just said. Lord Templewick went on. "You speak of her with utter disrespect, just because an accident has left her with a small but visible scar, which only shows just how poor your judgement is. You think her a woman with no options, and believe that you are the one with choices in life. You are wrong."

Jasper managed to laugh.

"I think not. Why do you say that?"

His voice was scornful. Lord Templewick smiled, and it was the smile of a man who had just been handed the opportunity he sought.

"I say that because of the fact that I have bought up all of your debts, Chater, every single one. I own you. I could call them all in, and leave you paupered, for I know that your father won't pay them. But more than that, I could make it known throughout society that you were that badly in debt, that you had no honour, that you weren't good for your vowels, and that no man should ever trust your word again. Even if your father did choose to pay, he could not undo what that would do to your reputation."

As he spoke, Jasper had gone pale, and then positively grey-faced.

"No... You can't... I don't believe you."

"Oh I can. Think yourself lucky that I don't plant you a facer right now for your arrogance as well." Templewick dropped Jasper unceremoniously, then reached into his coat, and pulled out a pile of papers. "See – every single vowel you owe against, all signed over to me – and there is a second copy with my man of business. You will leave my house within the next two hours, and you will speak of this to no one. And you will never touch, threaten, or hurt Lady Venetia and her mother again, in any way."

Chapter Seventeen

Morgan had listened at the door before entering, just in case there was something he should know before walking into the room – and he was so very glad that he had taken that precaution. His anger had risen, moment by moment, as he heard the words spoken between Jasper and Lady Venetia. The man was the lowest of the low, and deserved nothing more than to be felled by a punch, and locked away somewhere. But, satisfying as that might be, it was not a long-lasting solution – unlike the one provided by the papers in his pocket.

When Jasper spoke of making Lady Venetia his mistress, and then she screamed, Morgan could bear it no longer – he had heard enough to damn the man. He had thrust the door open, and surged into the room, to find that Jasper had Lady Venetia pinned beneath him, but before he could reach them, Jasper emitted a strangled half scream, and convulsed – from, as far as Morgan had been able to see as he crossed the room, the impact of Lady Venetia's knee in a sensitive place. He had grasped Jasper by the shoulders, pulled him off the Lady, and flung him to the floor.

He had then seated himself beside Lady Venetia, reaching instinctively to comfort her, and when she had leaned into him, he had kissed her brow, unable to help himself, feeling a desperate need to ease her discomfort, to protect her. That action had driven Lord Jasper to rouse himself to sneering commentary.

What had followed then had only partly gone according to his plan – he had used the leverage granted him by those papers to send Lord Jasper away, and to protect Lady Venetia and her mother, now and in the future – but in the midst of his tirade against the reprobate, he had made a very unplanned declaration of willingness to marry Lady Venetia.

Doing so had startled him, as much as it had obviously startled Lord Jasper, and Lady Venetia, but he'd had little time to consider it, so focussed was he on demanding what he wanted of Lord Jasper. After he'd stated his demands, Lord Jasper had stood there for a moment, shaking with what looked to be impotent fury, and now, after that fraught silence, he spoke again.

"You're a devil, Templewick, and one day I'll make you pay for this. But for now, it seems I have no choice." He turned to look at Lady Venetia, his face a picture of ugly dislike. "As for you, my slatternly cousin – you were never worth this, I should have known that nothing good could come of going anywhere near you. Templewick is welcome to you, and I wish him all the misery you can inflict on him."

With that, he rushed from the room, still a little unsteady after the force of her knee. The door slammed on his exit, and suddenly, they were alone, the ticking of the clock loud, the lack of all other sound somehow demanding that they speak to each other.

Despite that, neither spoke, although Morgan turned slowly to Lady Venetia. In that moment he realised that he had meant every word of that unplanned declaration – he would be happy to marry her, if she would accept his suit. It seemed so obvious to him now – she was the only woman he'd found any interest in spending time with, from the very start of their acquaintance, so the idea of marrying her should have been obvious – but even as he'd known that he was steadily coming to care for her more, his mind had not taken that final step – consciously, at least. It seemed that subconsciously it had, or he doubted he would have made that statement to Lord Jasper.

But how was he to begin speaking of it? What could he say about anything, right now? Then she solved that problem for him, by being the first to speak.

"My Lord... I... I must thank you again. But... how did you come to buy up Jasper's debts? And why? For that was surely a very large amount!"

He stepped forward, and took her hands. She blushed, but did not pull away.

"It was not insignificant – but it was certainly easily within my means. I regard it as a good investment, for what I have purchased is your freedom from his harassment. As to why... after what you told me, up at the ruins, I chose to act, in case such a situation as this ever arose – but in truth, I had not expected it to do so this soon."

She looked at him, and he realised that her hands were shaking in his grasp, and there was what looked suspiciously like the sheen of tears in her eyes. For a moment, her lip trembled, and he wanted, in that instant, to bend forward and kiss her – but would that not make him just as bad as Chater?

"I am overwhelmed by your kindness – in more ways than just that. Tell me, for I must know," her voice quivered, "what did you mean by saying that you would marry me? Was that something said in the heat of the moment, to contradict Jasper's nasty pronouncement? Or was it... of course, I would never try to hold you to such a thing, said at such a time...."

Her voice trailed off, and she looked away, embarrassed.

He considered but a moment, before laughing gently.

"Ah, I see – but what if I want to be held to it? If you'll have me?"

Her mouth dropped open in surprise for a moment, then closed a little as confusion filled her expression. Was she really so shocked that he might consider marrying her? Apparently so. He tugged on her hands gently, and pulled her close to him, then bent and pressed a kiss to her scar again. Her breath caught, and a small sob escaped her. He kissed her brow again, then trailed gentle kisses down her face until his lips found hers. She stiffened for a moment, and then, with a soft sigh against his lips, she melted against him, into the arms he encircled her with, and tentatively returned his kiss.

It was sweet, and heady, intoxicating in its innocence. It was a gift she gave him, and one which he would value, always.

A minute passed, and eventually he drew back, and met her eyes. She trembled in his grasp. Her voice when it came was barely more than a whisper.

"Thank you. But there is no need for you to be so kind... I would not have pity..."

That shocked him.

"My Lady, there is nothing of pity in that, nothing at all. I kissed you because I wanted to – I have wanted to, if I am truthful, almost since I first saw you. And the more time I spent with you, the more I came to care for you – but I did not know what you thought of me, and I was a fool, and said nothing to you of my feelings. All those weeks in London, and I never found the courage."

She laughed then, a sound with an almost hysterical edge to it, shaking her head.

"Then we have been fools together, my Lord, for I could say the same. The more time I spent with you, the more I liked you, the more I came to care for you. You were the only man who did not flinch from my face, who treated me kindly, always, yet I could not trust myself to believe that it might be anything more than kind friendship. I was too afraid that if I hoped for more, my heart would be broken."

He kissed her lips again, a butterfly soft brush, yet one which sent heat through him, as if he had been struck by lightning.

"Then let us be fools no longer, and explore what we have between us."

She nodded, and then, after drawing her lip between her teeth for a moment – which only made him want to kiss her again – she spoke.

"Then if we are to do that, there is a question I must ask you. Are you the man who sewed this," her fingers went to the scar on her brow momentarily, "with such neat stitches? For you look so like my faint memory..."

He was startled, all over again. He had not thought that, with the laudanum, and the blow she'd suffered to her head, she would have any memory of him at all, from that day.

"I... yes. I was that man."

She shook her head in bemusement.

"But... that man was a groom, come to collect a horse – how can it have been you? My memory of the day is faint, but still, you were so like, I have wondered – when you first looked on my face and did not flinch, I felt that it was almost as if you already knew the scar was there, as if you were not surprised..."

"In that you are right. I had heard that there was a young Lady with a scar, and when it was described to me, I was almost certain that it had to be the one I had repaired – so I was not surprised. I do apologise though, that I did not do a better job of stitchery, for the scar was still noticeable, and people have mocked you and treated you badly as a result. Please forgive me for the lack in my skills."

She shook her head.

"There is nothing to forgive. You are truly gifted – you did a remarkable job, after the utter mess I had managed to make of myself. Mother has always told me that I am too rash, that bad things would come of it, and she was right. If you had not been there, I would have had a far worse scar, and never been able to show my face in society again. And you know... I think that I am coming to like it, in a way. It is fading, so that the colour is now like a pale autumn leaf, as if one has tangled in my hair, and stuck against my face. Which is suitable, given the number of times I've fallen off horses into piles of leaves. But... I still don't understand why you were a groom..."

Morgan swallowed – this was the part where her aristocratic upbringing might make her disdain him – but, if they were being honest with each other, he must answer her. As if she knew his doubts, she gently squeezed his hand with hers.

"Generally, there are not many 'respectable' occupations for the son of a second son."

"But... you are Earl now?"

"Yes, only because my father has been dead for some time, and my uncle, who was his older brother, and Earl before me, died, with his wife, and all of their children, in the cholera plague of this past spring. I went into the military, when I was old enough, but I hated fighting. I learnt how to care for the horses, to heal them when they were injured, and from that, I was co-opted into the medical corps. I preferred healing men to fighting them. When I came home, I put those skills to good use as a groom, and then a stablemaster. I was so far from the line of inheritance for the title at that point, that I saw no reason to try to stay within the expected aristocratic behaviour – I chose to do something that gave me pleasure. So there I was that day, when you were carried in on a makeshift stretcher, with blood everywhere. All that battlefield experience took over – I just assumed command, told them what to do, and set about fixing you, because that was something I knew how to do. And now, as I remember it, I suspect that I have loved you from that moment, when, as they carried you in to the parlour, to set you on the table for me to work on your face, you opened your eyes and looked into mine. I fell into your gaze then, and I have never really escaped your thrall since."

She moved then, her eyes shining with tears, and rose on her toes to bring her lips to his.

"And I you. For I dreamed of your face, of your eyes, almost every night after I woke from the laudanum daze. I still do dream of it. I would wake from the dreams, and wish that you were real, were there with me, then I would get up and face another dreadful day."

"Then perhaps we should start today, to see what might truly be between us. But first, much though I would prefer to hide here with you, eventually someone will come looking for us, and I do not want to be found in a scandalous situation – not because I dislike being scandalous with you, but because I have no desire for any more nasty gossip. And also, we should make sure that Lord Jasper actually leaves within this next hour, and obeys my commands."

"We should. But thank you, again, for everything, from the moment you sewed up my face, to what you have done for me today."

*****

Venetia hurried up to her rooms, and stood before the mirror, not just to see what she might need to do to make sure that she looked perfectly respectable, but to stare at herself in wonder. He had said that he loved her! How could that be? Everyone told her that the scar had made her ugly, made her almost completely unmarriageable. Yet he had said....

She shook her head and two pins slipped free from a coil of her hair, allowing everything to collapse. She laughed then, broken out of her stunned state, and set about fixing it. Then she examined her dress carefully, and concluded that she should change. It was late afternoon by now, she realised, and her changing into a dress which would do for dinner would not surprise anyone.

She rang for Molly to help her change, but all the while that was happening, her mind was on Lord Templewick's words, about marrying her. *'If you'll have me'.* It had been said jokingly – hadn't it? She hadn't responded, because she hadn't known how to. Had that been, in actuality, a proposal? Would she be, even now, betrothed, if she'd answered? Or... did he actually think that they were betrothed, that her words afterwards were tantamount to an acceptance?

Oh! She was so confused.

But still, if he loved her, then surely everything could be sorted out?

Even so, it was going to be dashed difficult to sort it out – how does one casually ask a man if one is betrothed to him or not? Perhaps she would wait for him to say something, cowardly though that was.

Molly finished with all of her dress buttons, and then adjusted her hair, adding sparkly bejewelled pins.

"There you are my Lady, all pretty. Those amber coloured gems look so nice in your hair, and the necklace is lovely, I am sure that the other young ladies will be jealous."

"Thank you Molly, although I'm not sure that I'm actually pretty."

"Of course you are. You always have been!"

And with that, the maid hurried off to assist Lady Hardenwell.

Venetia contemplated the evening ahead, and realised, with overwhelming relief, that Jasper would not be there, that she could relax, and enjoy herself – unless, of course, Jasper had already succeeded in poisoning the minds of the other gentlemen against her. She would see.

*****

Morgan watched the rather shabby carriage drive off with satisfaction. It was the one and only hireable carriage in the local village, and as Lord Jasper had come with Wilborough, he'd had no choice but suffer the indignity of its aging springless structure. Morgan had paid for it, to make sure that Lord Jasper went as far away as possible, and as soon as possible. In fact, he'd overpaid, to ensure that the coachman wasn't bribeable by Lord Jasper.

His mind ran back over the events of the day – a most remarkable day, all in all.

A day on which he had realised that he loved Lady Venetia, and told her so. A day on which she had told him that she returned that love. A day on which he had declared his willingness to marry her, if she would have him. A day on which she had.... Not actually answered that implied question.

Damnation!

Tomorrow, early, he would have to find a way to ask her for an actual answer, before he proceeded with anything like wedding plans...

Chapter Eighteen

"Tonight is the Christmas celebration dinner. And tomorrow is Christmas Eve – when we must go home. I had so hoped that, by now..."

Lady Hardenwell sighed.

Venetia almost squirmed on her seat – what could she say? If Lord Templewick had meant his words as a proposal, and taken her acceptance of his kisses as acceptance of the proposal, then... but if he hadn't...

She swallowed.

"So had I. But at least Jasper is gone, and we don't have to put up with his company any longer."

"Indeed. Although it was very strange that he simple upped and left like that – it's most unlike him to walk away from free hospitality. I won't complain though – he is such a disagreeable man."

"He is – but he's gone, and we can enjoy tonight's dinner without his irritating presence. Perhaps, if we are lucky with the weather, I can get in one more ride with Lord Templewick in the morning, before we must leave."

"Yes. But for now, we'd best go down and see what people are doing."

After an hour in the beautifully Christmas decorated parlour, while people stared morosely out through the windows at the rain soaked countryside, and talked about the dreadful road conditions they were likely to experience on the way home, Venetia made quiet excuses to her mother and slipped out to go to the library – she was not going to let yesterday's events put her off using the room – there were too many wonderful books to explore in the short time that she was to be here.

As she walked along the corridor, past the top of the stairs, there was no one in sight – not even any servants. For a house full of people, it was very quiet. Then, as she came level with another door, it opened. She glanced sideways, to see Lord Templewick in the doorway.

He looked startled for a moment, then took one step forward, looked both ways along the corridor, turned back to her, and gave her the most wicked grin. And immediately took hold of her arm, and pulled her into the room, quickly shutting the door after her.

If it hadn't been for that grin, she might have been frightened. Instead, she was curious – what was this about? And... would it involve kisses? The thought made her pulse race, and her breath come short.

"My Lord! Just what is this about? This is, you realise, a shocking lack of propriety, for us to be alone together like this..."

"Is it? Because I might do this?"

With which words he drew her into his arms, and kissed her.

Everything else faded away, and she did not at all care in that moment whether anyone might find them in such a compromising position. All she cared about was the kiss. When he finally released her she stepped back, looked at him and simply said the first thing that came to mind.

"Yes."

"Yes? Is that yes to my question just now, or yes to my rather poorly delivered proposal of yesterday?"

"Ah... I... Was that a proposal, in truth?"

"Yes, it was. Will you have me, Venetia?"

Her world spun, and she put a hand out, grasping for something to steady her, and he took her arm. He had meant it – he had just asked her again. The tiny flame of hope that she had nurtured in her heart for all of these months burst into a raging fire. She was saved – saved from marring Lord Peterley, saved from being a poverty-stricken spinster, and instead, she was able to marry the man she loved.

"Yes, I will, with all my heart."

He pulled her into his arms again, and kissed her with a depth of passion which she had not known existed. She allowed it to sweep her away, losing all awareness of anything but him, of the kiss, of what had become her new world. Minutes later, they drew apart a little, both breathing hard.

"Thank you, Venetia – you have made me the happiest of men. Tonight's dinner can be our betrothal celebration, as well as a celebration of Christmas. But say nothing for now – I must speak with your mother, and make arrangements for all that will need to be done. And I will do that now, as soon as I possibly can, so that we can make our grand announcement at dinner tonight."

She nodded.

"Mother was in the parlour just before I came out. I was on my way to the library – so I will continue, and leave you to seek Mother out."

He raised an eyebrow.

"The library? Does not that bring bad memories, after yesterday?"

She shook her head.

"I can forget Jasper, in all his vileness, when that same library was the site of our first kiss, and of our first declarations of love. I will choose to remember that, always."

He bent forward and kissed her brow, his lips, for a moment, tracing the shape of her scar, then stepped back.

"I had best find your mother, then."

*****

When, many hours later, Lady Hardenwell had come seeking Venetia, she had found her calmly reading – well, from the outside she looked calm, but internally, it was a different matter.

"Venetia, my darling girl, I have just had a very long conversation with Lord Templewick. Before I do anything more, I must ask you the most important question. Do you truly wish this? Do you love him?"

Venetia lifted her head and met her mother's eyes.

"I do most definitely wish this, and yes, I love him – I think that I have from the first time I saw him, even though I did not know who he was, and he was then not an Earl at all."

Lady Hardenwell frowned.

"Not an Earl? What do you mean?"

"He didn't tell you? Mother, Lord Templewick was not always expected to succeed to the title. When we first met him, he was a groom, newly promoted to stablemaster. He is the one who sewed up my face on that terrible day. And I have dreamed of him ever since, even though I wasn't, after the laudanum, even sure if he was real. But he is real, and he loves me in return."

Lady Hardenwell dropped onto the seat beside Venetia.

"Well, that is a surprise. But so long as you are happy. We have already worked out the settlements, but I refused to sign until I spoke to you. I wanted to be sure. He is, I must say, an extremely generous man. Brightwood Chase will survive, and so will I. He has invited us to stay here through Christmastide, that we may all get to know each other better, without so many other people around us."

"That is wonderful. Will we announce this at dinner today, as he had suggested?"

"Yes. We will."

"Then I had best go up and prepare myself to look as beautiful as possible. This time, I will be the one being envied – and after the last six months of disdain, I will very much enjoy being treated differently."

*****

Morgan had spent part of the afternoon, after his long discussion with Lady Hardenwell, with his own mother. She had been delighted with his news, which was a great relief, but then she had looked at him with an amused smile.

"And have you thought what to give her, as a token of your betrothal? I have your grandmother's jewellery – my mother – and you also have all of the jewellery which was passed down through your father's family – it was in the personal items of your uncle and his wife. When we searched through everything, we found a concealed safe – and the man of business had a key. Why don't we look through it now, and find a ring or a necklace which you think will suit her?"

It was something he had completely failed to think of, but as soon as she said it, Morgan knew what he wanted.

"An excellent idea Mother. Is there, by chance, anything with emeralds?"

"I believe that there is."

"Then please, show me where it is."

An hour later, with dinner fast approaching, Morgan tapped on the door to Lady Venetia's rooms. The maid opened it.

"Might I speak to Lady Venetia for a few moments?"

"Of course my Lord, do come in and take a seat in the sitting room and I'll see if she's able to come out right now."

He went in, but could not settle to sit. Instead, he paced about the room, staring out through the window for a short while and being pleasantly surprised to see that the rain had eased.

After a few minutes, he heard the door to one of the bedchambers open, behind him. He turned away from the window, and simply stopped, struck dumb by Venetia's beauty. She was wearing a simple and elegant dress of pale green, decorated with fine silver lace, and with tiny green gems sewn in a pattern near the hem, and around the bodice. It was as if she had known what he would give her – which was impossible, as he hadn't known himself until an hour ago.

"Lady Venetia, I have a gift for you."

"A gift? Why?"

"To mark our betrothal." He went to the small table, and set the box down. "Please, open it."

She walked across to stand beside him, and the warmth of her body came to him, along with the delicate floral of her perfume. He forced himself to stand still and wait. She reached out a tentative finger and touched the worn leather of the box. Then curiosity obviously overcame her hesitance, and she gently lifted the lid. And gasped.

"They belonged to mother's mother – my grandmother. I thought the emeralds a perfect match for your eyes." He lifted the necklace from the box. "May I?"

"Yes."

He undid the clasp, and settled it around her neck, before making sure that it was securely clasped again. Then he lifted the bracelet and ring from the box.

"I don't know if the ring will fit – but we can get it altered if it doesn't."

But it did fit, perfectly, as if it had been made for her.

She looked at him with eyes which glittered with unshed tears.

"Thank you. You are so kind to me, I do not know what to say."

"You need say nothing. There is nothing to thank me for. It is only right that these should pass down to you now. But it is almost time for dinner, let us go down, and let people see just how beautiful you are."

*****

The closer she got to the parlour, the more nervous she felt. He had insisted that she should enter the room on his arm, with her mother close beside them. And she knew that, as soon as she did so, people would look, and draw conclusions, and begin to whisper amongst themselves. The thought made her shudder – she had already suffered enough of whispering to last a lifetime.

But when he gently squeezed her fingers, she looked up, and gathered herself. When had she become such a coward, she who had always been so rash and rushing into things with no fear? Mentally, she gave herself a stern talking to, and chose to again be that almost heedless girl, to trust her own instincts, and be damned what others thought.

She smiled, and lifted her chin, making no attempt to hide the scar on her face as they entered the room. A small silence followed, and then, as expected, there were some whispers. She ignored them.

They went forward, and she dropped her hand from Lord Templewick's arm, so that he might move about and greet his guests, whilst she and her mother went to join Lady Merringbar and some others. As soon as she possibly could, Amelia moved to stand close to Venetia, and whispered to her softly.

"Well, that was quite the entry. Do I take it from that....?"

Venetia attempted to put on her most innocent expression.

"Do you take what?"

Amelia sighed.

"That there is something between you and Lord Templewick, of course."

"At this point, I choose not to say anything."

"Ooooh! Well, that's good enough as a confirmation of my suspicions for me."

Venetia made a tutting noise.

"Stop making assumptions and have a little patience."

"So, if I must be patient, at least tell me for how long, or I shall die of curiosity."

Venetia laughed.

"I promise that you will know more before the end of this evening."

Amelia gave a huge sigh.

"Well, that's a relief."

They went on to talk of other things, but Venetia found her eyes following Lord Templewick about the room and every so often he would glance her way and smile, which filled her heart with joy. Eventually, after what seemed like an age, the butler came to the parlour door, and announced that dinner was ready. At which point, Lord Templewick came to Venetia, and offered her his arm, to lead her in to dinner.

Which was a very clear breach of protocol, for he should have been escorting the Lady of the highest rank present – which happened, now she thought about it, to be Venetia's mother. Whispers, of course, followed. She didn't care – the look in his eyes told her everything she needed to know.

In the dining room, the seating arrangement had her sitting on one side of him, and her mother on his other side. She simply smiled and sat. The dinner seemed interminable, even though the Christmas decorations made the room beautiful, and his cook had achieved marvels with the food. She could not, later, remember what they talked about, nor what she ate, for her mind was entirely on the moment which would occur after the dessert had been cleared away.

A moment which finally arrived. Lord Templewick stood, and called for everyone's attention. Venetia looked up at him, and thought, though he hid it well, that there was almost as much nervousness in him as there was in her.

He cleared his throat, and the room fell into silence.

"Ladies and gentlemen, this dinner was originally planned as a celebration of Christmas, but it has become much more than that. Today, Lady Venetia Chater has done me the honour of agreeing to be my wife. I ask you all to help us celebrate this joyous occasion."

There was a collective sigh of disappointment from nearly every young Lady in the room, and Venetia struggled not to laugh at their expressions. Then, as the shock of his announcement wore off, everyone started talking at once.

"Please, everyone, let us withdraw, ladies and gentlemen together, to the parlour, where there will be a glass of champagne in celebration, followed by sherry and port."

They rose, in far more disorder than would have usually been the case, and left the room, following Lord Templewick, who had Venetia on his arm again. The next hour was a complete whirlwind, as people came up to them to congratulate them, the girls all telling her how lucky she was, the men suddenly looking at her differently, as if the fact that one young man found her valuable enough to want to marry her had suddenly changed something.

Had it not been so ridiculous, it would have been funny.

Finally, the evening came to a close, and the ladies went upstairs to retire. Lord Templewick caught her hand as she made to leave the room, lifting it to his lips for a moment.

"Rest well, my love. Tomorrow, we will set everything in motion, so that we may marry as soon as possible – but first, we will have a peaceful Christmas together, just your family and mine."

She tightened her fingers on his, and leaned close.

"I love you."

And with that, she left him there to drink more port with the gentlemen.

*****

Morgan watched her leave the room, his heart full of love.

For a moment, he simply stood there, until Wilborough came up to clap him on the back again.

“And now, Templewick, in time honoured tradition, we gentlemen will help you to celebrate your coming nuptials by plying you with far too much good brandy. And you can tell us just how this came to be – for you’re a sly one, to have been quietly courting her without any of us realising!”

Chapter Nineteen

Christmas Eve was chaos, with all of his guests leaving, most of the gentlemen rather the worse for the indulgences in food and drink of the previous evening. The rain had stopped, but the roads were still inches deep in mud, so everyone would likely have a slow and frustrating journey. It was late afternoon before they were all gone. All, except, that is, Lady Venetia and her mother.

They stood with him, and his own mother, on the front steps, watching the last carriage disappear down the drive. He let the tension leave his shoulders, and gave a very loud sigh of relief. His mother laughed.

"Was it really that much of a chore to deal with them all, Morgan?"

He turned to her with a grin.

"Of course it was. You never raised me for all of this – no one ever expected me to have to deal with it. I'm not sure that I will ever feel comfortable in this life. I'll always be sneaking off to the stables, and pretending I have no greater responsibilities."

Venetia laughed then.

"And I will be beside you, in complete agreement. Horses are so much easier than people."

Lady Hardenwell shook her head knowingly.

"She will be, and still most likely doing rash things all the time." Then she turned to look at Morgan's mother, and gave her own theatrical sigh. "I suppose that simply means that you and I will need to dedicate ourselves to the organisation of this wedding, or nothing will happen..."

Morgan's mother slipped her arm through Lady Hardenwell's and led her into the house.

"Indeed we will, for I can see now that our children have no idea whatsoever of what is required."

Morgan watched them go, leaving himself and Venetia alone together, the crisp breeze lifting the edges of her skirts. Then he turned to her, pulled her into his arms, and kissed her. A kiss which lasted quite some time. Eventually, they stopped, and simply stood for a moment, gazing into each other's eyes. Then Morgan gave a soft laugh again.

"Let us not disappoint them. I am sure that if we slip out early tomorrow, to ride across the hills, they will just shake their heads in the confidence that they were right. Let tomorrow be a day for us, our Christmas gift to each other. We can worry about everything else in the days that follow – we can be wed by just after Twelfth Night, and if it were possible to marry earlier, I would suggest that we do so – but with the roads this way, obtaining a special licence might take almost as long as waiting for the banns to be read!"

"I agree. Let tomorrow be for us. The few weeks that follow will be for our mothers, and then, when all of the fuss is over, we can get on with our life together – although I too would have been happier if we could have wed immediately."

At those words he bent and kissed her again, a soft kiss on her brow, caressing the scar which had brought them together, and then they went into the blessedly quiet house, ready for the joy of Christmas in the morning.

Epilogue

"Is everything right? Are the pins falling out of my hair again?"

"Everything is just perfect, Venetia – stop fussing. You are a beautiful bride, and you are about to marry a wonderful man. Now come downstairs – the carriage is waiting to take us to the church."

Venetia forced herself to step away from the mirror, to accept that she was as ready as she could be, and to follow her mother from the room.

The day was fine, the thin dusting of snow which still lay on the ground looked perfect, clean of any stain, as if the whole world was crisp and clean, just for her. The weak winter sunlight drew sparks of light from the snow, and from the icicles on some of the trees. All in all, it seemed magical.

The carriage wound down the hill and along the valley to near the village, where the small church stood, picture perfect in the landscape. When she had imagined marrying, she had always thought of London, or the church at Hard Abbey, never of something like this!

They drew up before the door, and she stepped carefully down from the carriage, the delicate skirts of her gown lifted up until she stood on the top of the church steps.

"Are you ready?"

Venetia nodded.

"Nervous, but ready – are you?"

Against all convention, they had decided that Venetia's mother would walk her down the aisle to Lord Templewick. She had no male relative she would wish to have there.

"I am, although this is something which I never once in my life imagined that I might find myself doing!"

"Then let us go in, for I am so happy to be marrying a man I love, not some old lecher. I can't wait."

They stepped into the church, and the small congregation turned as one to see her. But after that first moment, Venetia was not aware of them at all – her eyes were only for Lord Templewick, waiting for her. His eyes met hers, and it was as if she floated down the aisle, buoyed by their shared happiness.

*****

It felt like he'd been waiting forever. But, finally, the moment came when he knew, by the whispers which ran around the church behind him, that she had arrived. He turned, and met her eyes.

For a moment, there was nothing but that, her beautiful face, the scar clear to see, not hidden by her hair, or by face powder. Then, after a moment, she began to walk to him, her mother by her side, and he took in everything about her – the magnificent gown she wore, in a green like the first spring leaves, with an outer layer of near transparent fine silver mesh, embroidered at the bodice in leaf patterns done in tiny emeralds, and at the hem in the same leaf patterns, but done in shades of amber, gold, red and brown, as if all the leaves of autumn clung to her at her feet. They matched the look of her scar perfectly.

He was enchanted by it, by her, in every way.

She reached him, and took his hand. They turned to face the Vicar, who was a cheerful man, full of kindness, and happily married himself. He smiled at them, indulgently, as if he could see their love for each other at a glance.

The ceremony began, and passed, in somewhat of a blur for Morgan, as they each gave their responses where required. It was only when the Vicar finally pronounced them man and wife that it all became real to him. As they left the church after signing the papers, he was happy that they had asked such a small select group of people to join them – for the well-wishes of even that small number felt overwhelming.

He was very glad to step up into the carriage for the journey back to Templewick Grange, where the Wedding Breakfast awaited them. But the first thing he did upon the door closing, and the carriage moving off, was to pull Venetia into his arms, and kiss her. When they finally drew apart a little, he settled her against his side on the seat, his arm around her.

"I would be very happy to simply continue to kiss you... but if I am to manage to get through the day, I must harbour my strength..."

She laughed softly.

"I would be very happy for you to continue to kiss me too, but I suppose that we must behave until this evening, at a time when we might reasonably retire. We must allow our mothers their enjoyment of all of the fuss too. Although... I will permit myself just one small indulgence, before I try to behave for the rest of the day." And with that, she pulled his head down to her, and kissed him. It was a tentative kiss which became certain, a kiss which promised much for the future, and set his blood aflame. Then she pulled back with a smile. "And that will have to sustain me until later."

"No rash impetuous actions today?"

"No more – I am sure that marrying you is quite enough rashness for now."

He shook his head, amused, and then they arrived, for the distance from the church to Templewick Grange was short, and they both turned their attention to dealing with the rest of the day.

*****

It was early afternoon, and everyone was relaxing in the parlour, after the Wedding Breakfast, replete with food and drink, and happiness. Venetia settled on the couch beside her mother, who smiled.

"I have some news for you. When we returned from the church, there was a letter waiting for me, from Brightwood Chase. Our estate manager wrote to tell me of his progress with all of the repairs to the tenants cottages, and to the House, using the funds which your wonderful husband has provided. You will be pleased to know that everything is well under way, and none of our tenants will suffer, going forward. He has also set about buying replacements for many of the items which we sold – so when you visit, it will be as it originally was. He has arranged to send your two horses here, next week, and asks what you would like the Housekeeper to pack up of your belongings and send. I know that you will want to come to Brightwood Chase soon, and arrange most of your things yourself, but you must ask now for at least enough to see you through the next few weeks."

"I will have to think about exactly what I want. But that is wonderful news about the tenants, and restoring the house to what it was. I will admit that I have been feeling dreadfully guilty, ever since my fall, as I watched the contents of the house diminish. Now, I can relax, knowing that you will be well off, and that all will be as it should be."

They spoke for a little longer, then both went in search of other conversations.

*****

Morgan felt exhausted by the day, but at last, the evening drew to a close, and he took Venetia's hand and led her up the stairs to the suite of rooms which they would share. She had asked that he not show her those rooms until now, even though she had been here, in the house, for she had wanted it to be a surprise. He hoped it was a pleasant one, for, while he had redecorated the rooms upon his arrival here, he had done so to his own taste...

"My Lady, I present to you, your new home – the more intimate part of it."

He opened the door, and ushered her in, closed the door behind them and simply stood and waited for her reaction. She paused, looking around her.

"Oh, this is lovely! Blue and cream is so restful."

"I am glad that you like it. This, as I am sure is obvious, is our private sitting room. The door to the right leads into my bedchamber – a room which I hope you will share with me, the majority of the time, and the door to the left leads to the bedchamber which is yours, to use as you wish. Each has an attached dressing room, and from them, connecting rooms with entries from the servant's corridors, for my valet and your maid."

She turned to him.

"Oh! A maid! Now that I am married, I cannot steal Molly from Mother – we will need to employ a Lady's maid for me."

He pulled her to him, and kissed her brow.

"We will, but tonight, I shall be your ladies maid." She blushed at his words, but made no complaint. "But there is one more thing which we should discuss – Mother reminded me, yesterday, that in the rush of things, with all of the Christmas celebrations, we never considered whether we would take a Wedding Trip."

"We didn't, did we? Do you want to?"

"I have some thoughts on the matter – but do you want to? Is there somewhere you would especially like to go?"

She shook her head.

"To be completely honest with you, I have never considered it – I am ashamed to admit that, in the desperation of the last six months, as long-term poverty seemed more and more likely, I had never thought beyond the need to marry. What would happen after that, I did not consider."

"Then, perhaps you will like my suggestion. I think that we should wait, and take a trip come summer, when the weather is better, and there are foals on the ground. We can buy more horses for our breeding establishment..."

"Breeding establishment? Do we have one?"

Her eyes sparkled as she asked the question, and he was sure that she knew the answer...

"No, but we will have, and soon."

They both, at that point, fell into laughter, and each other's arms. She looked up at him, her eyes bright.

"Then shall I lead you astray, and encourage you to make rash purchases of beautiful horses, and do slightly unwise things?"

"You may certainly lead me astray all you like, my darling Venetia – the idea delights me. Do you know – you are nothing like the woman I expected to have to marry, all for duty to the title, yet you are exactly perfect, for me, and for Templewick."

"And you, my love, are nothing like the man I expected to have to marry, just so that I, and my mother, could survive, yet you are perfect for me, in every way. I do not know how I came to be so lucky, but I am grateful, every moment of every day, for that fall, and this scar, for, without that happening, you would never have seen my face, or I yours, until we were both in London. Things would have been very, very different. I love you, more than I can say."

"And I love you, in equal measure."

He took her hand, and tugged her forward.

"Now, let me show you the bed which I hope you will share with me."

They went through the door to the right, but she barely had time to look around the room, before he scooped her up into his arms, carried her to the bed, and almost fell onto it with her.

"That's enough talking – now is for kisses, and more."

The End

About the Author

Arietta Richmond has been a compulsive reader and writer all her life. Whilst her reading has covered an enormous range of topics, history has always fascinated her, and historical novels have been amongst her favourite reading.

She has written a wide range of work, from business articles and other non-fiction works (published under a pen name) but fiction has always been a major part of her life. Now, her Regency Historical Romance books are finally being released. The Derbyshire Set is comprised of 11 novels (9 released so far). The 'His Majesty's Hounds' series is comprised of 17 novels, with the last now released.

She also has a number of standalone novels released, and four other series of novels at various stages of release. She lives in Australia, and when not reading or writing, likes to travel, and to see in person the places where history happened.

Be the first to know about it when Arietta's next book is released! Sign up to Arietta's newsletter at

http://www.ariettarichmond.com

When you do, you will receive two free subscriber exclusive books - **'A Gift of Love',** which is a prequel to the Derbyshire Set series, and ends on the day that 'The Earl's Unexpected Bride' begins, and **'Madame's Christmas Marquis'** which is an additional story in the His Majesty's Hounds series.

These stories are not for sale anywhere – they are absolutely exclusive to newsletter subscribers!

Connect with Arietta:

Donate and support her on Kofi.com https://ko-fi.com/ariettarichmondauthor

Follow her on Amazon - https://www.amazon.com/Arietta-Richmond/e/B016GG1KJ6/

Like her Facebook Page - https://www.facebook.com/AriettaRichmondAuthor

Follow her on Twitter - https://twitter.com/AriettaRichmond

Follow her on TikTok - https://www.tiktok.com/@ariettarichmond

Follow her on Instagram - https://www.instagram.com/AriettaRichmond/

Follow her on Bookbub – https://www.bookbub.com/authors/arietta-richmond

Follow her on Goodreads - https://www.goodreads.com/author/show/14508806.Arietta_Richmond

Here is your preview of

The Duke's Christmas Vow

Arietta Richmond

Prologue

Christmas Day 1816

"Your solemn vow, Rafael. Give me your solemn vow that you will find a suitable woman to marry, before next Christmas Day."

Rafael Livingstone, Duke of Oakmoor, regarded his mother with an expression compounded of frustration, resentment, and resignation. They were barely a week out of their year of mourning for his father and, already, it had come to this. He knew that he should marry, and get himself an heir, that it was part of the responsibility which came with the title, but he had hoped for a few years respite from the London Season, and the hovering hopeful young women who wished to be a Duchess.

Mourning had allowed him to avoid their shallow falsity for a year, but now, it seemed that there was to be no further escape.

"Surely, I can take a little more time about it? I would prefer to find a woman I might actually like, or even love, rather than simply tolerate! And I've yet to meet one. Every young woman of the *ton* that I have met is vapid, insipid, shallow, self-serving, and prone to gossip and lies. I abhor gossip, and dishonesty is just completely unacceptable."

"Nonetheless, I want your solemn vow. There must be one woman among them that you can tolerate. You cannot waste time – you need an heir. The thought that, if anything should happen to you, the title and estates would go to your uncle, is enough to make any sane person feel quite ill. Your uncle is incapable, bedridden – the estates would fall into disrepair, and everything that your father and his father worked for would be lost."

Rafe, nodded, unable to dispute her point. What she said was true. He swallowed, facing the fact that he would have to give her what she wanted, that duty bound him despite his personal misgivings. He would give his vow, and pray that a miracle happened, that somehow, he would meet a suitable woman, who was also pleasant, honest, straightforward, and had at least a modicum of intelligence.

"All right Mother. I give you my vow. By next Christmas Day, I will find a woman to marry."

"Thank you. But I warn you, don't take this lightly. If, by November, you have not become betrothed, I will organise a Christmas House Party, and you will choose from amongst those who attend."

Rafe shuddered.

"I will do my best to prevent it coming to that."

Chapter One

December 1817

Lady Charity Pemberton breathed deeply of the crisp wintry air. There was a touch of the scent of the sea to it, for Oakmoor Chase was close to the coast, a vast estate of forest and moor, which ran from rolling hills to dramatic sea cliffs. It was beautiful, in a stark kind of way. Above her, sea birds wheeled through the clouded sky, crying their mournful cries.

She felt a kinship with them, as if they cried for what they would never have, as she had often done. She shook her head. She should not be maudlin – the day was beautiful, she had already found a number of wonderful feathers, and it was nearing Christmas. The fact that she was at a Christmas House Party, where she knew no one else, and at which her mother desperately hoped she would attract the attention of the Duke strongly enough to get him to court her, should not be allowed to spoil her pleasure in the day.

Determination filled her. She would do her best. She needed to marry well, if she possibly could, for her family was, although titled, rather poor.

Still, the thought of conversing with the Duke sent chills through her.

She was hopeless at acceptable social conversation – she was far too honest, too blunt, too prone to answering questions before considering what would be the most polite thing to say. And, whilst she was by no means ugly, she was not beautiful – she was, instead, ordinary, and only stood out in company because of her dreadful dark red hair.

She pushed those thoughts aside with a sigh – there was nothing she could do to change any of it.

Both sides of the lane she was walking down were lined by high hedges of holly bushes, blocking the view of the fields beyond. The ground beneath her feet was crusted with frost, which crunched at every step, but there had been no snow for days. Ahead of her, she could see that the lane turned, but she could see no further than that bend. She would, she supposed, discover what was there, as soon as she reached that spot – but right now, she stopped – for, caught in the prickly leaves of the bushes, high up, was a magnificent, brilliantly white feather – from a gull, she suspected.

She carefully set down her small, covered basket, and stepped as close to the hedge as she could, without suffering too many pricklings from the leaves, and reached up for the feather. She was too short. Her fingertips were still inches below it. She tried jumping, but her pelisse snagged on the leaves, and she nearly fell. Carefully untangling herself, she tried again.

She still failed to capture the feather, but this time, as she dropped back towards the ground, she collided with something, hard.

*****

Rafe had risen before dawn, and slipped out of the house to walk across the fields, and along the cliffs. The crisp air shocked him fully awake, and sight of the dawn above the sea was familiar and reassuring, reminding him that beauty still existed, naturally. A reminder he needed when he currently had a house full of young ladies whose beauty was so artificial as to seem almost theatrical.

Now, he was striding down the lane, going back towards the house. If he was not visible in the breakfast room soon, his mother would nag at him again. It was his own fault, he supposed – he had vowed to her that he would find a woman to marry by this Christmas, but the year had gone by alarmingly fast, and here he was, still not betrothed, and therefore holding this damned house party.

Just the thought of it ruffled the calm he had achieved. He walked faster, almost charging around the bend in the lane – and ran straight into something – someone… instinctively, his arms went out, to catch whoever it was.

And that made it instantly apparent that it was a woman. Her back was to him, and his arms had ended up around her waist. The front of the skirts of her pelisse seemed to be entangled in the hedge, and her rather plain bonnet was askew on her head. That fact revealed a mass of curling dark red hair which was quite magnificent. Which also tickled his nose.

He moved, carefully adjusting his grip on her, and reached out with one hand to untangle her skirts from the hedge. Thus released, she turned in his arms, which meant that she was almost pressed against him, face to face.

Deep violet toned eyes met his. For a moment, he forgot to breathe. There was nothing artificial about the face before him. No cosmetics enhanced it – it was perfect, just as it was. Her lips, as naturally dark red as that hair, parted in surprise, and she blushed. He should release her – such an intimate hold on an unchaperoned young woman he did not know was well and truly beyond the bounds of propriety.

But he did not. Instead, he had the shocking urge to kiss those lips which were so very close to his.

"I… I'm sorry… I was… I fell…"

Her voice was as natural and beautiful as the rest of her. But it jolted him out of his daze, and he rapidly released her, first making sure that she was stable on her feet.

He stepped back a pace, putting a safe distance between them. A tiny frown crossed her brow, as if she had not wished him to move – but that was a silly conceit – no woman would want to be unceremoniously manhandled in a country lane.

"There's no need to apologise. I was thinking, walking too fast, and not looking where I was going. I am sure that you would have been quite all right if I had not collided with you."

She blushed again, and turned her eyes away from him for a moment.

"If I had not been distracted, I might have seen you coming, rather than being in a position to be collided with."

He looked at her – distracted? What did she mean? What had she been doing? There was nothing here but the frosted ground of the lane, and the high hedges bordering it.

"Distracted? What were you doing, that distracted you, and got your skirts caught in the hedge?"

She blushed again, a deep red, seeming intensely embarrassed, then lifted a hand to point upwards. At first, he had no idea what she was pointing at – then he realised that there was something white, stuck amongst the leaves, quite high up.

"I... I was trying to reach the feather. Sadly, I am too short to do so – and being holly, it's not the sort of hedge I can scramble into..."

Rafe felt his eyebrow rise – why would she want a feather? But he did not ask – it was none of his business, and if the Lady wanted a feather, there was no reason she shouldn't have it. He reached up, carefully extracted it from the prickly leaves, and presented it to her with a bow.

She took it with a curtsey.

"Thank you. I... I'll be on my way now. I am sorry for disrupting your walk."

She scooped up a small, covered basket, which he had not noticed until that moment, slipped the feather into it, and set off down the lane. He stood and watched her go, bemused, and more than a little intrigued.

She rounded the bend and disappeared from his view.

He had no idea who she was. And suddenly, that felt like a bad thing.

He shook his head, and set off again, walking as fast as he could, but now paying far more attention to his surroundings.

*****

Charity stopped as soon as she had gone a little way past the bend in the lane.

She was shaking.

That had been... she was almost certain that had been... the Duke. The man whose house party she was attending, with her mother. The man her mother hoped would find her so attractive that he would want to marry her.

And he had discovered her leaping about in a country lane like a small child, chasing a feather. She was mortified.

It was bad enough that she was plain, that they couldn't afford a better quality of gowns for her, that she was awkward in social situations, but now, she'd made the kind of first impression on a man which almost certainly guaranteed that he would find her laughable. No one understood why she collected feathers – in fact, almost no one knew that she did. Nor did they know what she did with them.

For what she did was perilously unrespectable, for it amounted to partaking in trade. The fact that the money she made from it was necessary to their survival at times did not make it any better. In the eyes of the *ton*, if it became known, she would be a pariah.

Once the shakes settled, she walked on, taking her time before returning to the house, lest she come across him again. At least he had not mocked her for her childishness in seeking a feather, or her foolishness in getting herself caught on the hedge. And he was, of a certainty, the most handsome man she had ever seen.

His attire had been of the best, yet simple, of plain colours and sturdy construction. And that moment when his eyes had met hers, as she stood in the circle of his arms - just the memory of it made her blush again.

He had looked at her as if he found her desirable. Which was quite the most wonderful thing which had ever happened to her.

She laughed at the thought. It had been disastrous, and wonderful, all at the same time. But she had best make sure that she was perfectly presented this afternoon, that she pretended their meeting had never occurred, and that she prayed he did not tell others of it, as an anecdote to laugh about.

That thought made her shiver with fear.

Her family depended on her – she had to marry well, and soon, or, after two years of poor crops, their crippling debts would become impossible.

Her father was far older than her mother, and an invalid – if she did not marry before he died, she was not at all sure what would become of them.

Yet... most men frightened her, in one way or another. Some were overbearing, arrogant and domineering, others were foppish, strange in their habits, and quite disturbingly odd. She needed to find a man who was not only someone she could countenance spending time with, but one who would not mind the near vanishing smallness of her dowry, and one who might help support her mother, when her father's inevitable death arrived and his title, as well as all but a few properties, went to her uncle.

She turned, and made her way back in the direction of the house, finding another three feathers along the way, and determinedly set her mind to forgetting all about being held in the Duke's arms.

*****

The breakfast room was full. He felt as if his mother had invited every unmarried woman in the *ton* to this House Party.

They fluttered about, all watching for any chance to place themselves in his path. Their mothers and fathers watched them, hopeful. The other men who attended – mainly brothers of the women, and a few who were actually his friends – watched the women, attempting, he suspected, to ascertain which ones Rafe wasn't interested in, so that they might consider them for themselves.

It made eating a peaceful breakfast an impossibility. There was no way to eat even something so simple as toast and marmalade, and still carry on vaguely polite conversation. So he said as little as possible – let them think him rude – and escaped to his study as soon as he could, despite the glare his mother gave him as he left the breakfast room.

Continued....

I hope that you enjoyed this preview!

Read the rest at:

Books in the Regency Gothic Series

Books in the A Duke's Daughters – the Elbury Bouquet Series

Books in the His Majesty's Hounds Series

Claiming the Heart of a Duke

Intriguing the Viscount

Giving a Heart of Lace

Being Lady Harriet's Hero

Enchanting the Duke

Redeeming the Marquess

Finding the Duke's Heir

Winning the Merchant Earl

Healing Lord Barton

Kissing the Duke of Hearts

Loving the Bitter Baron

Falling for the Earl

Rescuing the Countess

Betting on a Lady's Heart

Attracting the Spymaster

Courting a Spinster for Christmas

Restoring the Earl's Honour

From Soldier Spy to Lord (Books 1 to 3 as a set)

To Love a Determined Lady (Books 4 to 6 as a set)

Love Heals a Lord (Books 7 to 9 as a set)

To Love a Dashing Lord (Books 10 to thirteen as a set)

For a Lady's Honour (Books 14 to 17 as a set)

The Barrington Saga (all books related to the Barrington Family)

Books in The Derbyshire Set

The Earl's Unexpected Bride

The Captain's Compromised Heiress

The Viscount's Unsuitable Affair

The Count's Impetuous Seduction

The Rake's Unlikely Redemption

The Marquess' Scandalous Mistress

The Marchioness' Second Chance

A Viscount's Reluctant Passion

Lady Theodora's Christmas Wish

The Derbyshire Set Omnibus Edition Vol. 1 (the first three books all in one)

The Derbyshire Set Omnibus Edition Vol. 2 (the second three books all in one)

The Derbyshire Set Omnibus Edition Vol. 3 (the third three books all in one)

Books in the Regency Scandals Series

Books in the Nettlefold Chronicles

Regency Collections with Other Authors

Love in Autumn

A Regency Christmas Proposal

Love, One Regency Christmas

Love, One Spring Season

A Regency Romance Summer Collection
Regency Summer

A Regency Romance Summer Anthology
Regency Summer Secrets and Soirees

A Regency Christmas Together

A Regency Romance Christmas Collection
Regency Christmas Delight

A Regency Romance Summer Anthology
Regency Mid-Summer Mischief

A Regency Romance Christmas Anthology
Regency Missives and Mischief

A Regency Romance Summer Anthology
A Regency Summer Garden

A Regency Romance Christmas Anthology
A Regency Christmas Doubled

A Regency Romance Summer Anthology
Regency Summer Scandals

The Her Duke Collection

Themed Regency Collections

Other Books from Arietta

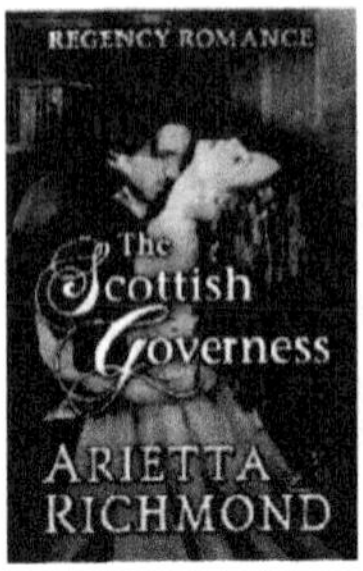

Regency Colouring Books

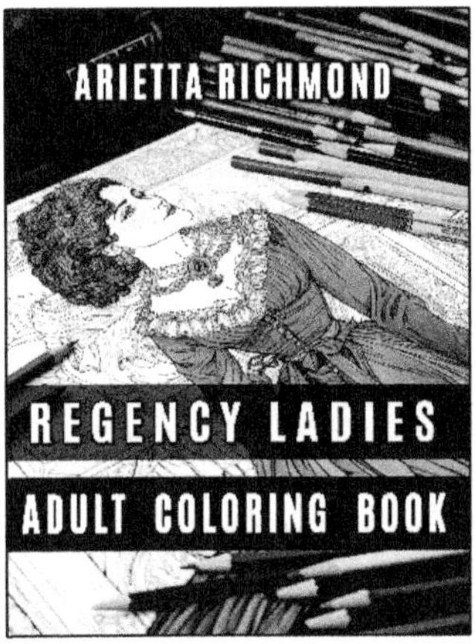

More coming soon!

Other Books from Dreamstone Publishing

Dreamstone publishes books in a wide variety of categories ranging from Clean Romance to Erotica, to Kids Books, Books on Writing, Business Books, Photography, Cook Books, Diaries, Colouring books and much more. New books are released each month.

Be the first to know when our next books are coming out

Be first to get all the news – sign up for our newsletter at

http://www.dreamstonepublishing.com

DREAMSTONE PUBLISHING

Printed in Great Britain
by Amazon

59610850R00126